WEB OF EVASION

When Lara Denton's unmarried mother dies in a horrific horse-riding accident, she is brought up by her only relative, Grandma Emma. However, when Lara becomes a jockey, Emma disinherits her. At twenty-five, disenchanted by the male dominated world of horse racing, Lara decides to return to Bingham and make peace with Emma. Sadly, she has died. Too late, Lara realises nothing is more important than family. But who was her father? Can she unravel the mystery surrounding her birth?

GLENIS WILSON

WEB OF EVASION

Complete and Unabridged

LINFORD
Leicester

First published in Great Britain in 2004

First Linford Edition
published 2005

British Library CIP Data

Wilson, Glenis
    Web of evasion.—Large print ed.—
Linford romance library
1. Fathers and daughters—Fiction
2. Love stories 3. Large type books
I. Title
823.9′14 [F]

ISBN 1–84395–935–6

Published by
F. A. Thorpe (Publishing)
Anstey, Leicestershire
Set by Words & Graphics Ltd.
Anstey, Leicestershire
Printed and bound in Great Britain by
T. J. International Ltd., Padstow, Cornwall

This book is printed on acid-free paper

1

'No way was I becoming the mistress. I'm not being any man's second best.' Lara filled the heavy dog dish with water and set it down firmly with a hollow thud on the caravan floor. Jodie, her golden retriever bitch, lapped gratefully. Theirs had been a long, hot drive from Ross Agarth's racing stables in Newmarket up to Melton Mowbray.

Kate Armstrong eyed her friend sympathetically, noting the lines of strain. She lit the ring under the kettle.

'Why did he think you would?'

'Because Ross was on a promise to apply for my jockey's licence, from the Jockey Club. He knew how desperate I was to get it. That was the reason I took the job.'

'Why the desperation?'

'In a few weeks I'll be twenty-five. You have to get a licence by then or

1

you've had it as regards being a professional jockey.'

'I see.' Kate nodded understandingly. 'But this racehorse trainer, he was a married man?'

'Too true. But I didn't know to begin with.'

'Trial separation?' Kate probed gently.

'Something like that, I suppose. Obviously, the grapevine was working. When his wife heard he was trying to woo me, she was back like a boomerang.'

'How did he react?'

'Only suggested we could see each other in secret.'

'Tricky, seeing as you work for him.'

'Did do,' Lara corrected. 'It was either being his mistress, an also-ran with no self-respect, or saying goodbye to a licence and leaving the job.'

'So, you left the job.'

'Left the job, left the tied accommodation and now I've dumped myself on you, hoping you'll be merciful and put me up whilst I sort myself out.'

Lara was acutely aware of the scorching flames of devastation from the bridges she'd burned. There was no denying she was in a dreadful mess. But if her world was a crumbled ruin around her ankles, her self-esteem was sky-high.

'That question doesn't need asking, and you know it,' Kate said flatly. 'You've nowhere else to go. Come on, you haven't any family, I mean, apart from your grandma, and we've been friends since we were kids.'

'Grandma Emma doesn't want to know,' Lara said, and the old scar tissue gave a nasty twinge.

It was nine years now since the wound had been inflicted and each time she thought about her beloved grandma the pain of their separation bit deeply. Resolutely, she shut out thoughts of her only relative. She had to, the memories were far too painful.

'So, that's settled,' Kate said, handing Lara a mug of tea. 'I insist, you and Jodie must stay here as my guests. Stay for as long as you wish.'

Following a surprisingly good night's sleep, Lara's energy level and spirits had lifted although, unfortunately, it hadn't given rise to the solution to her problem. But at least the question of accommodation could be shelved temporarily, thanks to Kate. Given the selfish uncertainty of the world, Kate was the most dependable of friends, a real star.

Lara, sitting by herself in the caravan nibbling a slice of toast, felt a surge of gratitude towards her. How fortunate she was to have such an unselfish friend. There was no-one to interrupt her thoughts right now because Kate was down at the farm helping with the milking. Lara recalled her words yesterday. Stay as long as you wish, she'd said. How many people would have made so generous an offer?

And simply because Kate had said it, Lara knew she must act quickly and resolve her problems. If not, the seductive temptation to drift, take advantage of the offer and let Kate cushion her would be too great to resist.

So, what mattered most to her? Lara knew she had to be unflinchingly honest with herself. For the last ten years that answer would undoubtedly have been her career. But now, was horse racing still her priority? Did it mean more to her than anything else? Lara took another bite of toast and chewed mechanically. She couldn't deny that she had become disillusioned with racing. The buzz and the satisfaction had all but disappeared.

With this new perspective which had been thrust upon her, she could see she had been incredibly selfish. She had stupidly spurned the unconditional love of the one person who really mattered to her. That depth of love wasn't to be found anywhere else but within a close relationship, and all relationships contained both pain and pleasure. If it hurt, which it did, to be reminded of their estrangement, surely that was a strong indication she should try and put an end to the hurt, for both of them.

What was her next step? The answer was blindingly obvious. She needed to be reconciled with Grandma Emma now, before it was too late.

The surge of joy inside confirmed her decision was the right one. The only question mark was whether Grandma Emma would accept the olive branch and welcome her.

Unexpectedly, Kate leaned in over the half-door.

'The mail's just come. I met the postman down at the farm and thought the letters might be important so I scurried back. There are two, for you. Must go, some of us have to work.'

She turned and disappeared but not before Lara had seen the flash of embarrassed annoyance in her friend's eyes. Despite her situation, Lara smiled ruefully. Right now Kate could prob-ably kick herself for being so thoughtless and insensitive. Not only was Lara jobless but homeless as well.

The letters lay at Lara's feet. They hadn't had far to travel — an eighteen-foot caravan didn't give much scope for aerodynamics. It didn't give much scope for two women living in it either, however good their relationship. Lara knew they would both heave sighs of considerable relief when she found somewhere else to lay her head.

Picking up the letters, Lara checked postmarks. The first one was from Newmarket in Suffolk and the second, Nottinghamshire. But the second one had been redirected firstly from Lambourn in Berkshire, where she had previously been working, and secondly from Agarth's Stables in Newmarket. The original posting date on the envelope was ten days ago. Who lived in Nottinghamshire who would bother to write? There was only Grandma Emma, and Lara had long ago given up all hopes of ever receiving a letter from her. So, who else? She couldn't think of anyone.

Conversely, she could think of plenty

in Newmarket, many who were friends and others she'd rather forget. When you worked — she had to amend that thought, too — had worked in horseracing, it was the nature of the job that you met an awful lot of people and it was impossible to get on well with them all. But she needed to forget her racing ambitions, let the past be just that and build a new future.

However, the letter from Newmarket not only bore the postmark it was printed along the top **Ross Agarth Racing Stables**. The writing seemed to mock Lara, almost as though it scorned her ability to let go, leave racing behind. But she had to and the loss was as grievous as a bereavement.

A cold nose pressed against her hand as Jodie sighed and laid a head on Lara's knee. There was a half-circle of white showing as the dog rolled her eyes upward to look into Lara's face. It was Jodie's way of saying she knew Lara was feeling down and was doing all she could to sympathise.

Lara gently pulled one of the long, silky buttermilk ears.

'Good girl, everything's all right.' Jodie gave a half-hearted wag that clearly said, if you say so, but I don't believe you.

Decisively, Lara opened the Newmarket envelope and drew out the single sheet of headed paper. With firmly anchored-down feelings, she read the half a dozen or so typed lines. It was very businesslike. Her P45 was enclosed and she wasn't to forget, if she wanted a reference, Ross would be pleased to supply one. He confirmed Lara's racecourse pass had now been returned to the Jockey Club.

Lara had a sick feeling as she read the letter. It took very little to sum up the end of her racing hopes and dreams, those dreams she'd held since childhood of being a successful lady jockey, until the harsh facts had finally impinged on those dreams that it was still a man's world in racing. True, there were ways of getting rides, like if you were a trainer's daughter or had relatives in racing. OK, you still had to have the expertise in the saddle but the almost impregnable iron door that stood between stable girls and the requisite jockey's licence was opened fractionally. You didn't have to keep on banging your head against the cold steel, until finally the reality that it was hurting too much and getting you nowhere penetrated.

Putting the Newmarket letter to one side, Lara picked up the second letter. It was from Jenkins, Jenkins & Pratt, Solicitors, and if the letter from the racing stables had rocked her, this one finished the job and knocked her flat. Opening it, she felt shock rip through her as she read the stark words.

We are sorry to have to inform you of the sudden death of Mrs Emma Denton on July 27.

Grandma Emma was dead! Lara's world came to a full stop. The letter fluttered from her fingers. No chance now of their reconciliation, not ever, it was too late. She was too late.

Lara felt a wrench inside as her emotions scorned rationalised thoughts and did their own thing. Whoever had likened it to a knife turning inside had certainly spoken from personal experience. Dry-eyed, Lara covered her face with both hands and let the pain ease away from her but even after the keenness had gone, her physical body felt weakened.

A nudge at her knee finally drew her attention. Jodie had retrieved the fallen letter from underneath the table and was holding it in her soft mouth.

'Good girl, Jodie,' Lara whispered, and took the letter.

Wincing as she re-read the dreadful first paragraph again, she forced herself to read the rest.

In accordance with Mrs Denton's last Will and Testament (copy enclosed) we are instructed to inform you, that you are the sole beneficiary.

Lara almost dropped the letter again.

Her immediate thought was she couldn't possibly accept anything. Taking a deep, steadying breath, she tried to think what Grandma wanted her to do. Logic kicked in. She herself may have been too late to instigate a reconciliation but her grandma hadn't been. By naming Lara as the beneficiary, Emma, even from beyond the grave, was effectively holding out the olive branch.

Lara read on swiftly. The entire estate, after payment of all outstanding accounts and testamentary expenses, had been bequeathed to Lara. It consisted of an eighteenth-century property, namely, Mounts Cottage, Bingham, Nottinghamshire, together with all outbuildings, stabling and grounds comprising in all three acres of land, together with approximately six thousand pounds.

There was a clause in the will that stated a condition that must be complied with. At this point, cynicism surfaced. She had been fooling herself, of course, thinking the last nine years could have been obliterated, even healed somehow, at a single stroke. Lara braced herself to read some damning clause that would sweep away all possibilities of her receiving the legacy, but, more importantly, by its inference, Grandma's forgiveness.

She continued reading, curious now to know what charity Grandma had chosen, not vindictively, but simply following through on her decision nine years ago to cut Lara out of her will.

But the clause was not what she expected at all. It stated that Lara allow Maria Ellahanta, Mrs Denton's executrix, to remain as resident in part of the estate. The letter ended with the solicitors saying they would be pleased if Lara would make an appointment to visit their offices to discuss her legacy at her earliest convenience.

Tottering across the tiny kitchen area, Lara groped for the kettle. She didn't take sugar in tea normally but the shock warranted it and she dropped two heaped spoonfuls into the mug. Although not in denial, she had accepted the dreadful fact that Grandma Emma was dead. Lara found herself unable to cry and knew her grief was not yet ready to be released. It was not so much the shock of being informed of the legacy that was creating such havoc with her emotions, as the staggering fact that Grandma had actually wanted her to have it.

Years before, at the time Lara had opted to go into racing against her wishes, Grandma had disowned her. But Mrs Denton, obviously, had since placed matters in the hands of the family solicitors, so it must be true. Lara gulped the nauseatingly sweet tea and mulled over the contents of the letter. Clearly, her next move was to go and see the solicitors.

Kate's battered old caravan, rented out by the farmer for whom she worked, didn't boast a telephone and Lara hadn't a mobile. The nearest public phone would be a couple of miles away in Melton Mowbray. Shakily, Lara scribbled a hasty note to Kate and pinned it down to the kitchen table with an empty mug. She clicked fingers to Jodie.

'Come on, girl.' The dog leaped excitedly down the caravan steps, tail waving in anticipation. They piled into Queen Victoria, Lara's stalwart 1965 Morris Traveller, and went in search of a public call box.

Finding one on the outskirts of Melton, Lara lifted the receiver and, licking dry lips, dialled the solicitors' number. How ridiculous it was to feel so unsure of herself. This was the first step towards a new future.

The receptionist, oozing reverence, said, 'The earliest Mr Jenkins Senior will be free for an appointment is tomorrow, at eleven-thirty. Do you wish to see him then?'

Lara fought down the threatening panic.

'Thank you,' she said, 'I'll take it.'

A delicious, savoury smell greeted

Lara as she entered the caravan. Kate was curled up in the window seat, her hands cupping a steaming mug.

'Help yourself. It's vegetable soup. Why did you have to ring a solicitor? Are you suing Mr Agarth for wrongful job description?'

'It's a thought. I could even amend it to blackmail, couldn't I?'

Lara ladled out a mug of soup. She retrieved both that morning's letters and handed them to Kate. Reading the Newmarket one first, Kate snorted and tossed it onto the seat beside her.

'Don't let that one concern you.'

Lara slid on to the long seat beside her.

'Agarth and the job are history. I've already moved on.'

Kate, hand hovering over the second letter, glanced at Lara.

'And this one?'

'Read it,' Lara replied and Kate did so.

'Oh, no.' She bit her lip, shaking her head. 'Lara, I'm so, so sorry.'

16

'Thanks.' Lara's voice was barely above a whisper. 'And do you know what?' She gulped. 'I'd just decided this morning to make it up with Grandma. I was calling a halt to this stupid separation.'

'And now it's too late. How awful.'

They sat in silence. Neither had much appetite left.

'You're going back, though?' Kate asked.

'Looks like it.'

'What will you do for a living?'

'I've no idea,' Lara said ruefully. 'Horses are all I know.'

'It's such a pity you've no other relations.'

'Yes. And that's something all this has taught me. The value of family.'

'But too late,' Kate commiserated.

'Maybe, maybe not.'

'Why? What are you getting at?'

'My mother was someone's mistress, Kate. If he's still alive, I must have a father somewhere.'

'Without being unkind, it's unlikely

you'll ever trace him, even if he is all the family you might have.'

'Look, Kate, I've learned my lesson. I've lost Grandma. If I hadn't, I'd never have come to this decision. I realise now just what I've thrown away. If there are any other relatives, family, any-where, I'd like to find them. But, of course, the one I really need to find is my father.'

'Have you thought, he may not even want you to? Could be embarrassing for him, for both of you.'

'I'll risk it,' Lara said. 'Even if he doesn't want me, I must try to find my original roots.' She smiled sadly. 'Don't you see, Kate? I have to, for my own identity and my peace.'

Tuesday was a scorcher. Having driven all the way from Melton Mowbray, all the shady parking spaces had been taken in Bingham carpark, but she was lucky, as there was one space left.

Messrs Jenkins, Jenkins & Pratt, Solicitors still occupied the same offices in Market Street as they had when the firm began some eighty years ago, at the time Mr Jenkins Senior's father had first established a practice in the town. Lara had no need to ask directions. Her formative years had been spent here in Bingham, her schooling begun at the infant school, and finished at Nottingham High School.

Crossing the carpark, Jodie walking obediently to heel, Lara turned into Market Street, her thoughts still on her childhood. She must have been a great disappointment to Grandma Emma. Most pupils on finishing at the High School went on to university. Lara knew Grandma had already, in her own mind, seen her do just that. But well before the age of thirteen, Lara longed only to have school over on Fridays and the weekend in front. Against Emma's wishes, she spent most of it at Pegasus Racing Stables, which was only about a mile from Mounts Cottage where they lived.

Lara's thoughts were interrupted by

her arrival outside the Georgian bow window with the name of the solicitors painted above it. She glanced at her watch. She was three minutes early. A bell tinkled as the door opened and the receptionist looked up from her desk, smiling enquiringly.

'Miss Denton. I have an appointment with Mr Jenkins.' Lara could have left it at that but some imp inside made her add, 'Mr Jenkins, Senior.'

'Oh, yes. The late Mrs Emma Denton's estate, isn't it?' Before Lara had a chance to confirm or deny it, she flicked a switch on the internal switchboard and said reverently, 'Miss Denton is here, sir.'

Mr Jenkins, Senior, in his inner sanctum, was sitting behind a huge mahogany desk. The size of the desk dwarfed him even after he had risen to his feet and stooped forward to shake hands. His gold-rimmed glasses slid gently down his nose.

'So nice to see you again, Lara. Do be seated.'

It must have been about nine years since Lara had last seen him, when he had made a house visit to clear up some legal matter for Grandma, but he seemed hardly changed at all. He expressed genuine sympathy over her bereavement.

'Thank you,' she said, somewhat touched by his old-world courtesy. 'Could you tell me anything about her death? You see, we'd lost touch such a long time ago. I didn't even know she'd been ill.'

'Family relationships are among the most complex,' he nodded understandingly. 'Mrs Denton suffered a severe stroke, apparently, and subsequently died shortly afterwards.'

'Have you any idea what might have caused it?'

'I understand that preceding the onset of the stroke, she did have a visitor. I certainly couldn't say if the visit contributed to the cause of the stroke, you understand.'

'I certainly wouldn't ask you to

express an opinion on it,' Lara said, well aware that shutters were already closing over his face. 'It would be extremely unethical.'

He smiled at her and nodded.

'Quite so, quite so. Now,' he said briskly, 'regarding your grandmother's will. It contains a clause giving rights of occupation for as long as she wishes to a Miss Maria Ellahanta. These rights do not pertain to Mounts Cottage itself, but to a conversion of part of a stable loft that was constructed some eight years ago, since when Miss Ellahanta has resided there rent free. You do understand that to comply with your grandmother's last wishes, Lara, you would have to allow Miss Ellahanta to remain unless, of course, she herself decided to leave.'

'Who is this lady? Do you know anything about her?'

'Yes, well, I did ask your grand-mother similar questions.' Mr Jenkins straightened up and sat back in his chair, fingertips making a pyramid in front of him. 'Mrs Denton informed me Miss Ellahanta was an old and trusted friend she'd known from her youth, both having gone to the same school. Apparently, Emma was somewhat lonely after your departure and Miss Ellahanta returned from abroad at the same time. The two events coinciding, your grandmother offered a home to Miss Ellahanta.'

'I see. Is she retired? I suppose she must be.'

'The best thing to do would be to meet Miss Ellahanta, unless of course,' he hesitated a moment, looking steadily at her, 'you've already made an alternative decision regarding the clause in the will.'

'Circumstances seem to have made the decision for me, Mr Jenkins. If Grandma truly wanted me to return to Mounts Cottage, then I shall do.'

'Excellent!' He gave her a beaming smile.

'I only wish I had done so earlier, whilst my grandma was still alive.'

'Yes, yes indeed. However, she'd be pleased to know you are returning home to look after the property.'

'I intend to. I'll go and see Miss Ellahanta this afternoon.'

'I shall require a copy of your birth certificate and there are some necessary documents to be signed, formalities, I'm afraid.' Dipping into a file, he drew out a small, sealed envelope. 'Amongst her papers, your grandmother left this letter addressed to you.' He passed across the envelope, together with a set of keys on a key ring, and also a separate sheet of paper. 'Perhaps you could sign this receipt for them both, between the two pencilled crosses, please.'

Lara signed obediently and slipped the letter into her shoulder bag. It was something so personal it needed to be read in private, the first letter in nearly nine years, and she certainly didn't wish to break down in his office.

'When did my grandma make this will?'

'That's one fact I don't need to verify. Emma made the will on the occasion of her sixty-fifth birthday. She had a small gathering for drinks. I, myself, was invited. However, she asked that I arrive a short time before the other guests in order that she could make clear her wishes regarding the disposal of her estate.'

'Grandma always did have a sense of occasion.'

'She did, didn't she? However, she instructed me very firmly I was to release the keys to you immediately, should you wish to return home, of course.'

He rose to his feet. Lara, taking the hint, pushed back her chair. She shook his hand.

'I'll let you have my birth certificate as soon as I can. Thank you very much for all your help, Mr Jenkins.'

'Not at all, my dear. Your grandmother would be delighted, as I am, that you're coming back home.'

Bright sunshine swamped her as she

left the office and walked Jodie back down Market Street. It was only just noon and she didn't want to turn up at Mounts Cottage until after lunch. Miss Ellahanta would otherwise, no doubt, feel obliged to offer her a meal and Lara didn't want to impose on their first meeting.

There was a dog walkers' paradise on the outskirts of Bingham and the problem could be solved by taking a picnic and also letting Jodie have an amble along Cuckoo Walk. Lara had made sure she'd packed a fresh bottle of water and the dog bowl in the back of the car before they set off this morning. Jodie could have a drink at the car both before and after her walk.

Seeing a bakery shop, she went in, leaving Jodie on a stay command outside. She bought a salad-filled roll and a boxed drink of blackcurrant juice. It would keep her going until this evening when she returned to Melton.

However, her earlier nervousness at seeing the solicitors had transmitted itself in the usual manner and there was only one thing which she simply had to do — urgently.

Back at the car, she poured Jodie a drink and then popped her into the rear of the car. The driver's window had, as usual, jammed about twenty centimetres from the top, enough to allow sufficient air in whilst she slipped across to the public conveniences at the far end of the carpark.

She'd been gone less than five minutes and was hurrying back to Queen Victoria when she noticed a man standing by the car. As she drew closer, the man straightened and put hands on hips. She would have thought him ruggedly good-looking, with his dark curly hair and wide shoulders, if he hadn't been looking so furious.

He glared at her. 'How dare you leave her all by herself.' His whole body language spelled anger. 'You are the only person she's got.'

Lara's heart began to thump uncomfortably. She didn't need anybody to compound the guilt she felt about her grandma.

'It's utterly despicable.'

'Are you talking about Emma?' she asked in a low voice.

'Of course.' His eyes blazed. 'But it's quite obvious, you have absolutely no conscience. How could you be so uncaring? She's an old lady.'

2

'Instead of standing there staring at me,' the man said acidly, 'I suggest you get Emma out of the car immediately.'

At his words, relief flooded her. Of course! She ought to have realised. He wasn't talking about Grandma at all. He'd been speaking in the present tense. It was a stupid misunderstanding triggered by her over-sensitivity at losing Emma. But since visiting the solicitors, inevitably, Grandma had been at the forefront of her mind, dominating her thoughts.

'We've got our wires crossed.' She smiled at him. 'This isn't Emma. My dog is called Jodie. I didn't realise you were talking about leaving her in the vehicle. I know she's not a young pup anymore, she'll be eight at Christmas, but she's fully fit and I've only been gone five minutes, if that.'

His eyes narrowed. 'And I'm supposed to believe you?'

'Yes, because it's the truth.'

'But how do I know that? You're a stranger. Why should I trust you?'

'Look, you don't seriously think I'd leave a dog in the car on a hot afternoon like this, do you? The car would turn into a cooker.'

'Well,' he said sarcastically, pointing to the driver's window, 'no doubt you would call that adequate ventilation, I suppose.'

'Excuse me. I certainly would not.' Lara, annoyed now by his arrogant attitude, opened the rear door and clicked fingers to Jodie who leaped down. 'But I'm not going to stand here and argue with you any further.'

Fastening the leash, she locked the car.

'Don't think you can get away with this sort of thing,' he snapped. 'I shall be looking out for you again, and the dog.'

Lara turned on her heel, ignoring

him, feeling mortified that anyone would think her capable of inflicting suffering on Jodie. She marched away across the carpark, diverted through the cut-through and came out on to Fairfield Street. Crossing over at the lights, she walked up to the crest of the hill, slowly now, the sun hot on her shoulders.

A wooden stile by the side of the road led into a tiny, wooded triangle. Here, it was blessedly cool, the thick canopy of leaves effectively blocking out most of the heat from the sun. A steep, zigzagging pathway led downwards on to what used to be a railway branch line, no longer used now by anything other than feet and paws. The original lines and sleepers had been removed long ago and the narrow path, no longer mundanely straight, meandered between bushes and trees. Nature had had a field day and luxurious growth cloaked the steep banks.

Lara released Jodie and she bounded ahead happily, but it was far too hot to do much running and the dog soon returned to walk by her side. Lara strolled slowly along, remembering with pleasure the countless times in her childhood and early teens when she'd run, played, slid down the high banks covered with frost-crisp snow, climbed trees or simply exercised the dogs in this little earthly paradise.

They had always kept dogs at Mounts Cottage. Grandma had been dog-mad all her life. She had also been horse-mad, until the accident involving her daughter, Esther. The horrendous accident that killed Esther had also robbed Lara of a mother she had never known.

A wood pigeon suddenly clattered out of the branches of an ash tree, startling Lara and thankfully stopped the running spool of memory. She didn't want to think those bleak thoughts, not now when her world was encapsulated in this green and golden pathway with the hot sun beaming down from an impossibly blue sky. The atmosphere was one of soporific peace and she drank it in greedily. Peace was something that had been lacking in her life for far too long.

She walked on through the long tunnel scrunching on the rough gravel which covered the ground inside it and listening to the amplified sound echoing down to the far end. Jodie's ears pricked up and she pranced nervously.

'It's OK, girl,' Lara soothed and the acoustics caught the sound of her voice and flung that down the tunnel, too.

Overhead she could hear the muted rumble as a heavy lorry passed by. The tunnel took the re-routed traffic away from Bingham in a cross direction with the new bypass that had been con-structed since she'd last lived here. Doubtless, it meant that the village itself whilst not returning to its original sleepy state of years ago, would at least be spared the worst volume of traffic.

They reached the far end and emerged into the blazing sunshine. Jodie trotted ahead, pleased to be out in the open again. They walked on under the next bridge and came to the third. Here the path widened into a big circle and a large, fallen log served to provide seating, partly in the sunshine and partly under the shadow of the bridge.

Lara flicked her fingers to the dog and sat down in the shade. Together, they enjoyed the contents of the lunch bag and Lara sipped the blackcurrant drink through a straw.

Jodie flopped down contentedly at her feet, head on paws, comfortable in the coolness of the bridge shadow, but not sleeping. Her eyes watched the path where it wound away ahead.

Lara leaned back against the old bricks of the bridge and closed her eyes. Even the birds were taking a siesta and were silent. She was filled with a sense of having returned home, and a growing sense of awareness that she had done the right thing, coming back, even if the man she'd spoken to in the carpark had been less than welcoming. It was a pity they'd met like that. On reflection, she admitted, had circumstances been different, she would have found him an attractive man. She was on the point of dozing off when a low woof from Jodie jerked her to full consciousness.

A dog had appeared round the bend of the path and was shortly followed by a second. The first one, a young collie, bounded forward and sniffed noses delicately with Jodie. Contact established, both tails began to wag and Lara waved Jodie away.

'Go on, have a scamper, enjoy yourselves.' And they did, dashing around each other, tapping forefeet on the ground challenging one another to play.

Lara looked towards the second dog, which had now almost reached her. It reminded her of a dog Grandma Emma had had years before, a black Labrador, but a vigorous two-year-old. This one, now sniffing her leg, was an old boy, getting a little stiff in his joints with age. Her hand went up to him and scratched the area beneath his throat. A shining disc lay against the thick black hair and she gently turned it over and read his name, Dusty.

A feeling of déjà vu came over her. She supposed it was possible, just. She'd been gone almost nine years, which would make him eleven. Grandma's dog had been called Dusty. In fact, she had named him herself on the very day he arrived. Pup-like, he'd been full of curiosity and exploration and had found the coalhouse door ajar. He'd thought it a fine game to go in and scramble up and down the coal heap, emerging later so covered in coal dust only his eyes were clean.

'Dusty?' Lara questioned softly.

The old dog stood back and gave a couple of tremendous barks, then he wormed his head firmly under her arm-pit and made low, moaning woofs.

Tears filled Lara's eyes, she couldn't stop them, didn't want to. She'd forgotten this trait of Dusty's. Always, after she'd been away for even a few hours, he would burrow close to her and make these peculiar noises of pleasure at seeing her again. It was Grandma's old dog. Lara knew him and he had recognised her. Although she had let the chance of seeing Grandma slip away, to be welcomed by her old dog somehow healed the rift that had existed all these years. Lara hugged the Labrador tightly, tears running unchecked down her face.

'Emma would have been so glad,' a woman's voice said.

Lara scrubbed a hand across her face, self-consciously removing the tears. A small, elderly woman, wearing a blouse of brightest blue over a long cream skirt, stood in front. Her feet were bare inside leather sandals. Her hair was the most striking feature, long, so long it reached her waist, and tied back in a thick plait. Lara found it hard to judge her age, but the blackness of the plait was at variance to the hair caught back from her face. Complete strands of it springing from her temples were silver.

'I'm pleased to meet you, Lara.'

She held out a hand. Seeing Lara's bewilderment, she gave a chuckle that sounded like water trickling over stones in a stream.

'Emma spoke of you, not to begin with, but latterly. I think it was in her mind to contact you, had she lived.'

Lara stood up, releasing herself from Dusty and took the proferred hand.

'You're Maria?'

'I am.' Deep-set dark eyes smiled at her.

'You and Grandma must have been close friends.'

'Indeed.'

'You must miss her,' Lara said, impulsively, still holding the thin hand.

'Yes, I miss her earthly presence, but that is a human reaction, of course, merely self-sympathy.'

'I don't quite . . . '

'Just my way.'

Without expanding further, she turned and whistled the first dog, which came to heel obediently, panting heavily.

'Good boy, Tippy.' She dropped a hand and smoothed his head. 'I don't usually walk them at this time of day but I was delayed this morning.' She spun on her heel, caressing Jodie. 'You are coming back with us to Mounts Cottage, aren't you?'

'Yes, please. I was coming to see you after lunch.'

Maria nodded as she walked away. 'Yes, I know.'

Disconcerted, Lara called Jodie and they followed the tiny, erect figure back along Cuckoo Walk.

The paddock-cum-orchard of Mounts Cottage joined the boundary of Cuckoo Walk about a quarter of a mile farther on. Climbing the high bank using the roughly-made and much-worn indents as footholds, they came to the cottage from the rear. The fruit trees were heavy with ripening apples and plums although the leaves were curled and dried by the weeks of unremitting sun.

'For the last three or four seasons, your grandmother used to organise a supplier and sell the fruit,' Maria said. 'We couldn't use it all and it was such a shame to let it waste.'

'Who picked them?'

'Adam Branston, my grandson. He's our local journalist, certainly not Emma and me,' Maria gurgled. 'Our tree-climbing days are long past.'

'I used to be quite good at climbing trees.' Lara looked up nostalgically into the branches above their heads. 'Guess I must have climbed all of these in my childhood. Don't know if I'd be any good at it now though, not since falling out of the hayloft. I've no head for heights any more.'

They walked on through the kitchen garden. The word cottage was a misnomer because it was a large, rambling property. Lara noticed the old brickwork had been re-pointed fairly recently and the Georgian window frames with small panes of bottle glass set here and there, looked to have been replaced as well. All the outside timbers were well maintained and smartly painted in a fashionable green. The overall effect was of a well-looked after and cared-for property, not a reflection of a depressed, embittered woman with nothing to live for. It spoke of an ongoing attitude to life that told Lara a great deal about Grandma. She would not have wanted to die. Lara wondered again who that fateful, last visitor had been. She was quite sure in her own mind that Mr Jenkins, Senior, knew very well who had called that day. Possibly, Maria knew, too. She intended to ask but not now.

Rounding a corner, they came into the stable yard with its L-shaped run of outbuildings and stables. Here again all was neat but with one essential missing — horses. Lara had a hollow feeling inside. Where curious heads in their direction were to be expected, there were simply shuttered doors.

The three or four top halves, which were open and bolted back, were blank, like blind eyes. The emptiness hit Lara harder than she'd have thought possible. Up to the time she'd walked out, there had been two or three horses in the stables. Thinking about it, Lara saw her grandma's thought pattern in that if she actually had access to horses, perhaps it would be enough to placate her from seeking a career in racing.

Maria was watching her, reading the emotion on her face.

'Emma told me she sold the horses after you'd gone.'

Lara managed a nod. Seeking to distract her, Maria pointed across the yard.

'I live over the tack-room. Come on, I'll show you.'

The original wooden stairway outside led up to a platform where a door allowed entrance into the loft. But as Lara saw on entering, it was no longer a loft used for storage. The entire length was utilised as one very large, long room, albeit with a screen partition near one end. Maria waved an arm encompassing the whole.

'I've lived here over eight years. It has all I need, all I want.'

Lara looked about. There was an electric cooker, washing machine, fridge and, tucked under one small, latticed window at one end, a single narrow bed covered with a hand-knitted patchwork quilt. Maria walked down to the screen and swung it aside.

'See, even a shower and toilet. I need nothing more.'

Lara looked at her, read the unspoken question behind her words and nodded.

'It's yours, until you no longer want it. My grandma wished it.'

Maria lifted her gaze to the ceiling and stroked a hand down the column of her throat, whispering, 'Emma's wish, yes, but what of your wishes?'

'I see no reason to oppose my grandma's dying request. Her judgement was very sound.'

'She was my best friend,' Maria said sadly. 'I miss her company.'

'I shall always regret never making that first move earlier.' Lara felt the catch of unshed tears. 'It should have come from me. Ironically, I'd already decided to come home, but now it's too late.'

Maria nodded. 'As you say, too late. Why do we stupid humans always leave it too late? It would alleviate all the if onlys.'

'And the pain.'

'Come,' Maria said abruptly, 'I'll take you over to the cottage.'

She took down a key from a hook against the sink.

'I go across every morning and open the windows.'

They walked past the empty stables and Maria unlocked the door of Mounts Cottage. Lara hesitated on the step, unsure of how she would feel to be back home again.

'Would you rather be alone?'

'No, it just seems a bit strange, that's all.'

Lara squared her shoulders and

walked into the kitchen. Very little had changed. The big cream Aga basking along one wall greeted her by its very familiarity, likewise the old, scrubbed, pine table at which she and Grandma used to eat most meals apart from dinner in the evening. Grandma had always been a stickler for the niceties of life and Lara had had to change, usually from jodhpurs, into a decent dress, before eating dinner in the dining-room.

Maria went through to the sitting-room. Lara followed and found this room, too, virtually unchanged. The fireplace was made of natural brick and an ornate, tapestry firescreen stood in front of the wide, empty grate. Grandma had worked the tapestry herself, many years before. A black worn leather strap hung down each side of the fireplace.

Spaced out at intervals were authentic horse-brasses. These had once hung upon the forehead and harness of the big Shires, belonging to Lara's great-grandfather. Their huge, feathered hooves would have tirelessly tramped the fields dragging behind the iron plough with its blades silvered by the constant bite into the firm, packed earth.

A great sadness filled her. If only Grandma had been able to accept that the accident that robbed her of Esther was quite simply that, an accident. But she couldn't. Over the years, the grief had slowly turned to a burning hatred against the cause of it — horses. Only one actually, but from then on they were all as guilty as the black stallion, Oliver, which had bolted with Lara's mother, galloped on to the local railway line and collided head-on with a tanker train.

The stunned train driver had later told how Esther had been pitched high and wide to land in the furrows of an adjacent ploughed field. The stallion was killed instantaneously. Esther died, too, a few hours later, but probably because of the softness of the newly-turned soil, the unborn baby she was carrying, cushioned by its placenta, had survived the impact. Doctors carried out a swift Caesarean, saving the baby's life. Lara had been that baby.

Looking at the horse brasses reawakened the memories and brought them rolling back in a tidal wave of shattering awareness. Her face must have mirrored outwardly the emotional shock waves because Maria stepped forward and touched her arm lightly.

'Sit down and I'll bring you some iced water. It will calm you.'

Lara nodded and sank thankfully into a leather winged chair.

'I guess it's everything rushing back so suddenly.'

Lara lay back gratefully, leaned her head against one of the high wings and closed her eyes. She had been totally unprepared for this onrush of emotion. Maria reappeared with a misted glass of water with chunks of ice floating in it.

'Sip this, child.'

Meekly, Lara took the glass and drank deeply. The coldness was exquisitely refreshing. Maria smiled.

'I feel the house is welcoming you back, reaching out to you. You belong here. Be still now, close your eyes and see if you can sense it.'

Lara took a deep, steadying breath. A tiny breeze fanned the curtains and they stirred gently before softly falling back into place. She closed her eyes. All was very still. The house seemed to have been holding its breath for a long, long time awaiting her return and had now sighed deeply with immense satisfaction and settled itself around her. She opened her eyes slowly feeling very dreamy, almost as if the cottage had put a spell upon her, and looked across at Maria.

Maria smiled. 'I see all I need to in your face. You have come home.'

'This is also your home,' Lara said as she rose to her feet. 'Would you like to move into the cottage with me?'

'My home is out there.'

Maria waved a vague hand in the direction of the stable yard.

'But I'd really like you to share the comforts of the cottage.'

'I have all the comforts I want, child. Your grandmother pressed me to share with her but . . . ' She shrugged as though it were of no great importance. Lara was about to argue when Maria continued. 'It gives my seekers the security they like. They would not find it here. My simple home is a reassurance of isolated privacy. And the vibrations are right.'

If she'd hoped to dispel Lara's bewilderment, it hadn't worked. Lara was really floundering now.

'I'm sorry, Maria, but I've absolutely no idea what you're talking about. What do you mean, your seekers?'

'I don't call them clients, nor customers. That is not the way I work. I prefer to say seekers, people who are searching for someone, some animal, something. What does it matter what they seek? I may be of help, or I may not. If they wish to give something voluntarily, I do not refuse, but I do not ask nor do I charge. It is of no consequence.'

Abruptly, she turned and walked out.

Through the window Lara watched as she crossed the deserted stable yard and climbed the steps to her personal eyrie above the tack-room. What Grandma had thought of Maria, she couldn't begin to guess. The woman was nothing like her own preconceived image. To say she was intrigued was an understatement.

She thought about Maria all the way back to Melton Mowbray.

3

Maria climbed the wooden steps to the loft and went across to the window overlooking the stable yard. Standing to one side, holding the edge of the curtain away from the window frame, she was able to view without being seen. Almost immediately, she saw Lara leave Mounts Cottage and walk away. She could see a renewed confidence about the girl, a firmness in the step as Lara walked out through the main gate headed towards the carpark, with Jodie trotting at her heels.

Abruptly, Maria let the curtain drop. 'So like Emma,' she murmured, tears starting at the back of her eyes, 'just the same proud tilt to her head Emma always had, that unmistakable touch of class. A thing I've never had . . . '

She lay down on her bed, letting the

long-held-back tears have their way as they trickled from beneath her closed eyelids. It was the first time she'd allowed herself to cry out the grief of losing her old friend.

True, there had been many low moments. One in particular, several days after Emma's death, she remembered vividly. On the point of breaking down, someone, a seeker, had knocked at the door, and she had put his need before her own. The man, old George Calledine, had been in a rare state over the disappearance of his aged terrier, Gyp. At sixteen, Gyp was past running off but something must have lured him away.

'Can you help me, lass?' George had stood at the door, twisting his grimy, old cap between equally grimy hands. 'I knows you've got the gift. You found May Kingsley's dog when she'd gone missing.'

In the face of his distress, Maria had swallowed her own grief.

'Come away in, George, have a seat.'

'You do find missing dogs, don't you?'

'Sometimes, not always. It isn't like a detective agency. I can't give you a guarantee.'

His face crumpled, 'Please, could you just try? My Gyp, he's an old boy, like me. Needs his heart pills . . . ' His voice trailed away.

Maria picked up the waves of anxiety.

'Calm yourself, George. It won't help to use negative energy. Tell me everything from the beginning. When did you lose him?'

George did so, ending, 'And I knows he's not the first to go missing. There was May's dog and Maud Jackson lost Tess on Cuckoo Walk an' all.'

'Do you have Gyp's collar?' Maria asked gently.

George nodded and handed it over, saying, 'Please do your best.'

Maria closed her eyes to shut out external distractions and let the leather dog collar slide through her fingers.

With hands clenched into tight fists,

George sat silent, willing her to come up with the answer.

'It would be better if you relaxed,' Maria murmured without opening her eyes. 'Tension blocks the vibrations I am trying to pick up.'

Obediently, George relaxed his hands, spread his cap across one knee and sat staring blindly at the toe-caps of his old boots.

For a few minutes, there was complete silence and then Maria began speaking.

'I am picking up a conflicting pattern. Gyp hasn't returned home, yet, but I think he's on his way back. He isn't far away. I see a path through the woods. It's Cuckoo Walk. Gyp's not walking, though, he's lying on grey stones, flints.'

'He's not . . . ' George's hands clenched into tight white-knuckled fists.

'No, but if we don't find him, he could well be.'

George lurched to his feet.

'He'll be needing his heart pills. Will

you come with me to Cuckoo Walk? Can we find him if we go and search together?'

Maria, eyes still closed, gave a brief nod.

'You must be prepared for whatever we might find.'

'Right.' He squared his shoulders. 'I promise I won't go to pieces on you, lass. But let's just go, now!'

George grabbed the collar and clipped it back on the lead. Maria watched and said nothing. There was a deep sadness within her. She felt very strongly that Gyp would not be needing it for much longer. But surely, wasn't it just possible she could be wrong?

She had had to be strong, put aside her own grief that day and had been repaid by the sight of the dog lying amongst the old flints from the original railway track beneath the fourth bridge along Cuckoo Walk. He was still alive. The relief on George's face as he had scooped up the little dog, held him close and stroked a rough palm across the wiry hair on the dog's head had been more than enough reward.

'Thanks, Gran,' Adam, her grand-son, said when he came round that evening to see how she was. 'George and his wife lived for each other. Since Annie died, Gyp's just about all he has left.'

Adam, so undemonstrative, had caught her cheeks between his palms and kissed her forehead. Maria knew he had a special affection for the old man but, even so, she was surprised by his gratitude. He was such a caring man, this grandson of hers, Maria thought fondly, as she smiled up into his deep blue eyes.

She had used the word grandson when describing him to Lara because that was how she thought of him, but in reality, only herself and two other people knew he was no blood relation. Adopted by her son, Jack, when he'd remarried after his first wife's death, they'd agreed to keep the secret from baby Adam and then somehow, the moment was never right to tell him the truth.

'I really do appreciate what you did for George, Gran, you know that,' Adam said as he smiled back at her.

'I'd have done the same for anybody.'

'I know you would,' he said softly, 'only this time it happened to be George.'

George had tried to press some money into her hand after they'd found the little dog, but she had waved it away.

'That's not what it's about. It's about reuniting those who need to be united.'

If only she and Emma could still be united.

Now, as she lay on the bed, crying, Maria remembered that day, which had truly been one of the worst in her life, and dashed away the hot tears. She'd had to be strong then, too, for Emma's sake.

The stable yard had been bathed in bright morning sunshine as she'd walked across to Mounts Cottage.

She'd intended to suggest to Emma they had lunch outside in the orchard and sample a new vegetarian dish she'd just tried out and found to be delicious. The kitchen door had been open and Maria tapped and went straight in. Until her dying day, she would never forget the sight of Emma lying helpless on the kitchen floor, both limbs on the left side like useless dead weights, her face twisted and drawn down. Only her eyes were the same, and they had looked beseechingly up at Maria, fear filled and holding an urgency within.

'Emma, my love.' Maria had dropped to the floor, cradling her friend's head. 'Hold on, I'll ring the doctor. What is it, what are you trying to say?'

And Emma tried, but the efforts of moving her mouth and struggling with the sounds had caused sweat to bead on her upper lip and forehead.

'Rest, rest,' Maria urged, dismayed at the effort it had cost Emma to utter the broken sounds. 'I'll try and guess what you want to tell me.'

Both Emma's eyelids had closed for several seconds before she'd again looked desperately up into Maria's face.

'Is it something you've left undone?' Both eyelids closed again. 'Good, good, take it very easily. Is there something you want me to do for you?'

Emma responded again. Maria wracked her brain as to what was so important.

'Is it Lara?' Emma closed both eyes again. 'It's the letters, isn't it? Yes, I know about them, my dear, those you've never posted. You want me to give them to her?'

Amazement and relief replaced the fierce burning in her old friend's eyes. With a shuddering sigh, Emma Denton closed her eyes again, but this time, she kept them closed. Maria lowered Emma's head gently on to the mat, then darted away to the hall, picked up the phone and called for an ambulance. Whilst she waited for help, she placed a soft pillow under Emma's head and wrapped a blanket about her. She kneeled down and felt the thin, fluttery pulse and prayed the doctor would hurry up.

Emma had been taken to the Queen's Hospital in Nottingham and Maria went with her. The doctor's diagnosis was not good. Emma must have been lying on the floor for some time before she'd been found. He pursed his lips, shaking his head a little.

'She must have an incredibly strong constitution or tremendous willpower, but I'm afraid she is deteriorating. I'm sorry it's just a matter of time. I suggest you go home and get a night's rest. If necessary, we'll ring you, but otherwise, try to get some rest and come back tomorrow.'

They'd sent her home in a taxi. But instead of climbing the steps to the loft, Maria crossed the yard and went into Mounts Cottage. There was something that had to be done. Going into the study, she took a tiny key from where it hung behind the ornate wall mirror and unlocked Emma's bureau. The letters were all tucked into one of the pigeon-holes. There were four. She had them in her hand, was about to close the bureau, and then hesitated. What should be done about the most important item of all? If anything did happen to Emma, the whole estate would doubtless belong to Lara. Legally, she would be in the wrong to take anything else, but apart from herself, no-one else knew what the bureau contained. Was it the right thing to do? Maria hesitated. Then, decisively, she snatched it up.

Locking the bureau and the cottage, Maria hastened across the stable yard and climbed the steps to the loft.

She undressed and lay down on her bed. Quite surprisingly, she had then slept. It was the telephone that awoke her shortly after seven o'clock the next morning. It was the hospital. There would be no need to visit. Emma had died in the early hours of the morning.

Suddenly aware now of the hot wetness of fresh tears trickling down her cheeks, Maria struggled to sit up. She brushed them away impatiently, cross with herself now. She had been so strong, until Lara's arrival.

'Emma, my old friend,' she whispered, 'I miss you. Wherever you are, I send my love.'

A gentle, cold nose pushed at her hand, licking away the salty wetness.

'Dusty sends you his love, too.'

She caressed the old dog's head. His tail wagged a contented acceptance and he walked stiffly over to his basket and flopped down. Maria kneeled down at the side of the bed and lifted a corner of the wool rug. A short length of one of the floorboards was loose and pressing down on one end, Maria lifted it out completely. Reaching down inside, she pulled out a package wrapped in plastic. Placing it on top of the bed, she carefully removed the wrapping. The package contained a dark oak box. Maria raised the carved lid. Inside was a very old leather-bound, family Bible. The box was constructed so that when the Bible was lifted out, it revealed a hollowed-out interior.

From this hollowed space Maria took out the four letters, all addressed to Lara. She must put them back in Emma's bureau before Lara returned to Mounts Cottage. But the cavity was still not empty. Inside were four other documents. The first one was Emma's marriage certificate, the other three all birth certificates belonging to Emma, Lara and Esther.

With trembling fingers, Maria lifted them from their hiding place.

'And what am I going to do with them, Emma? Am I to let the dead, and the living, keep their secrets? Or would you rather I gave them to Lara, let her open Pandora's Box?'

4

The cockerel's enthusiastic crowing roused old George Calledine from a restless doze. After the five pints he'd drunk last night at the Dog And Duck, two very kindly bought by Adam, sleep should have been easy. It would have blotted out the memory that today was the third anniversary of Annie's death. But some things beer couldn't blot out. It had proved a long, lonely night and George had only managed to doze fitfully.

Now, for a few seconds, he lay motionless, spread across the top of the old patchwork quilt, eyes screwed up tightly as if by so doing he could squeeze out the raucous noise. Down in the yard at the rear of the cottage, the cockerel drew in yet another deep breath, spread wide his black plumage and let rip. His harem of hens gave soft, chuckling clucks of approving admiration, shuffled their feathers and settled down again.

With great effort, George opened his eyes, looked blearily at the undulating ceiling and rolled off the bed. Groaning as his bare feet met wooden floorboards, he lurched to the window. Opening the casement wide, he bellowed at the offending bird. Considering it was barely light yet, he followed that by a remarkably well-aimed boot which cannoned off the side of the henhouse causing a flurry of commotion inside.

Closing the window with a bang which he instantly regretted, old George looked longingly at his bed but there was a job needing to be done, one in his own interests of self-preservation.

The cottage was one of a pair built nearly eighty years ago and used to house the farm labourers. Long past retirement, the old man was grateful to the farmer for allowing him to stay at a very modest rent. The farmer's wife often found a fresh rabbit outside. She didn't need to ask who had left it. On both sides there were never any thanks nor yet questions but old George's rent was never increased.

If the farmer disapproved of George's illegal methods of trapping rabbits, he never voiced it. The trap also supplied George with fresh meat. It supplemented his tiny pension because most of that passed from his hand to that of the landlord of the Dog And Duck down in the Market Place, except for the money he put aside each Thursday morning in an old tobacco tin. That was for the vet. It paid for heart tablets. It kept Gyp alive.

He'd set his trap before going to the pub last night. It was waiting out there in Cuckoo Walk. He had to check it before anyone else found it. George wobbled his way down the narrow stairs.

In the kitchen, Gyp staggered out of his basket and came to greet him.

'Now then, lad, how's it going? Better

with you than me, I hope.'

The dog licked his hand and clambered thankfully back into the basket, sighed, and fell asleep. George sucked his teeth and stood staring down at Gyp. If Gyp went, there'd be nothing left, and yet, despite the loneliness and all the heartache, life was still precious. If only he could just get on top of things once more, instead of feeling crushed down.

At the kitchen sink he turned on the cold tap. He never bothered to heat water in the tank. A kettle now and again was all he needed. Cupping hands, George splashed the cold water on his face, gasping at the shock and grasping for the dingy towel hanging on the line above the gas cooker. Burying his face in the rough fibres, he scrubbed the wetness away. He caught sight of himself in the spotted mirror above the draining board.

'Gawd, what a sight you do look,' he muttered, shaking his head.

Tossing the towel from him he thrust

bare feet into wellingtons and reached for the shotgun standing waiting by the kitchen door. On rare occasions he managed to pot a pheasant but that was something to be kept secret from the farmer. He tugged open the cupboard door under the sink. With trembling fingers he drew out a half-empty whisky bottle. George took a gulp. The spirit found the right spot and warmed his stomach.

Sighing with pleasure, he screwed the top back and set the bottle down on the cracked draining board. Grasping the shotgun, he turned to look at Gyp who had opened one eye.

'You'd better stay behind. Don't want you a getting lost again.'

George went out, banging the cottage door behind him and made his way along the cracked paving slabs to the hand-gate. The door bumped hard against the doorjamb, failed to latch and sprang ajar. Gyp, nosing the gap wider, hobbled painfully after his master. Beyond the gate, the rough track led through fields to Cuckoo Walk and George weaved his way along unsteadily. The initial glow in his stomach had left behind a sick, unpleasant feeling and his head began to spin ever so slowly. George stopped and rubbed a hand over his eyes. It didn't help.

At that very moment, he caught a flash of bright chestnut feathers topped with scarlet. It was a magnificent cock pheasant. Instinctively, his fingers gripped the gun. George felt a rush of excitement. He lifted the gun to his shoulder and tried to steady it. The barrel dipped and wavered. The pheasant stopped to peck and George, seeing his chance, squeezed the trigger. With a sharp alarm call and a mad flapping of wings, the cock pheasant tried to take off. Simultaneously, George saw a small brown terrier launch itself towards the bird. But as the pheasant became airborne and flew away, the terrier dropped heavily to the ground and lay still.

The gun slid from George's hands. He stumbled forward knowing even before he reached the dog that Gyp had chased his last pheasant. Infinitely gentle, he bent down, lifted Gyp and, cradling him close, shambled back the way he had come. Finally, he came to the cottage and going inside, closed the door. Gasping and sobbing, he leaned back against it finding some comfort in the solidness of the wood behind his shoulder blades as if it stood between him and a hostile world.

'Annie,' he whimpered, 'Aw, Annie.'

★   ★   ★

In the tiny flat above Bingham's newspaper office, Adam Branston turned over in bed for the umpteenth time. He sighed in exasperation. It was proving a bad night. He'd about given up hope of dropping off to sleep.

Six months after a divorce should surely have allowed time to adjust to sleeping alone, especially following such a short-lived marriage. Ten months was no time at all, except that it had given him a glimpse of what married life could be, or should be, like. Well, at least the first five months had. After that Julie's boredom threshold had breached its banks. She'd begun an affair with the estate agent's clerk and subsequently gone away with him.

Adam sighed and turned over yet again. Why did he keep on dredging it up? His mind kept away from the thoughts of Julie during the day but some nights, like this one, just the emptiness of the bed reproached him.

Just as he was considering the therapeutic value of getting a single bed, there was a distant, muted shot. Bird scarer from Cuckoo Walk fields, he thought. His mind registered the sound automatically and he counted five slowly and waited. Nothing happened.

Sitting up in the crumpled bed, he yawned widely, ran a hand through a thatch of dark curly hair and looked at the time by the bedside clock. It read five thirty-two. As he watched the red light clicked forward, five thirty-three. Strange, the bird scarer always gave two imitation gunshots with a five-second gap between them, but not this time.

Wide awake now, Adam gave up any lingering thoughts on sleep and went through to the kitchen for a mug of coffee. As always thoughts of work on hand for the day took control. He wondered if young Sophie Kettlewell might pop in with anything interesting on the local scene. He was a bit short of small news items for this Friday's edition of the Bingham's Own News. Young Sophie was a good, reliable and accurate little newshound.

He placed two slices of wholemeal bread in the toaster. Waiting for it to pop up, he pondered if he ought to increase her casual payments. She saved him a lot of work. The write-ups were hard enough without all the routine legwork. Sophie, herself, didn't seem to object. Her heart was set on becoming a journalist. That second-hand bike he'd bought for her had been an investment really. It saved them both time and effort.

Adam was not unaware that the money Sophie earned not only helped her, but also her mother, Mary Kettlewell. The toast jumped up and whilst he spread it lavishly with butter, he wondered what the new owner of Mounts Cottage would be like. Would she keep Mary on? Emma had employed Mary as a cleaner at the cottage ever since Mary's husband's fatal accident. It would certainly cause her financial hardship to find her services no longer needed. Biting into the toast, Adam nodded to himself. Yes, it was definitely time he increased Sophie's earnings.

Lara was sitting in the middle of the caravan floor surrounded by piles of clothing, books and CDs when Kate came in for lunch.

'Friday's not supposed to be a good day for moving house, is it?'

'Don't ask me.' Lara smiled and

stuffed an oversized T-shirt she used as nightwear into a holdall. 'And I'm not really moving house, just moving back home.'

'Why not stay a few more days?' Kate cajoled.

'I've stayed much too long already.' She waved aside Kate's protests. 'Honestly, look how much of your food I've munched. And you'll have twice the space when I've gone.'

'I've had twice the fun whilst you've been here.'

Lara pushed the holdall out of the way under the long window seat and going over to the cooker, took out two jacket potatoes, which she cut in half. Removing the middles, she mixed in a generous heap of red Leicester cheese, refilled the skins and set them under the grill to bubble and brown.

Kate sniffed hungrily.

'Besides, who's going to get my food ready when you've gone?'

'How about that boyfriend who turned up a couple of nights back? He wasn't as thrilled seeing me here as you seem to be.'

'Sam?'

'You've more than one?'

'Sam's only a friend, really. It's nothing serious.'

'If I were you, I'd make sure. The look in his eyes said given a chance he could get a real relationship going.'

'Well, maybe . . . Anyway, what about you? There might just be a fanciable man waiting over in Bingham.'

'And there might not.'

Lara slid the deliciously-bubbling cheesy jackets from under the grill and handed a plate to Kate.

'The only man I'm interested in seeing,' she said firmly, 'is my father.'

As Lara drove down Cherry Street into the market town of Bingham, the bells of Saint Mary's church pealed out sweetly. Early evening on Fridays had always been practise night for the local bell-ringers.

Grandma Emma had been a Bingham bell-ringer for over thirty years,

75

always on Friday nights and also whenever the occasion or the vicar called for it. Was she still taking an active part up until her death? Lara, negotiating Queen Victoria through the market place, felt a twinge of loss. How foolish she had been not to try and repair the rent between them.

There was so much that she had missed these last few years. Now she would never be able to fill in the blanks, or would she? Was it possible that someone might be able to help fit in the missing jigsaw pieces? Perhaps someone like Maria might know. Lara was determined to ask her. Even if Maria didn't know personally, she might suggest others who had possibly been close to Emma.

Lara drove through the open gates of Mounts Cottage and pulled up in the yard. It was sweet of Maria to have the gates open ready. Out of courtesy, she'd rung to say it would be just after seven when she arrived. She opened the rear door for Jodie who bounded out, feathery tail waving. The dog ran a yard or two towards the woman who was descending the outside wooden stairs. Lara raised a hand in greeting.

Maria called across, 'Welcome home, my dear. I've a casserole waiting in the oven. Come on up and share it.'

'Sounds lovely, thanks so much. I really appreciate it. I'll put Jodie in the kitchen first.'

'Nonsense. Dusty and Tippy are fully-fed and snoozing, another one will be no trouble.'

Halfway up the stairs, following Maria, Lara noticed a sporty-looking black car parked against the tack-room wall. 'Is that your car, Maria?'

'Car? No, I don't drive anymore.' She laughed lightly. 'Can't afford one.'

Lara was puzzled and about to enquire further when Maria opened the door to the hayloft flat.

'Here we are,' she announced as a man rose from the easy chair.

Shocked and dismayed, Lara took in the dark, curly hair, vivid blue eyes and wide, powerful shoulders. She had very much hoped not to meet the man from the carpark again and now here he was in Maria's home and obviously about to share the evening meal.

'Adam, let me introduce you to Lara,' Maria continued smiling. 'Lara meet Adam, my grandson.'

An intense, embarrassed silence descended. When it had stretched uncomfortably, Adam said, 'We have met.' His gaze never left Lara's face. 'Although, I didn't know her name was Lara, nor that she was Emma's prodigal granddaughter.'

5

'I'm certainly Emma's granddaughter, I don't know about the prodigal bit,' Lara said and to her chagrin, she felt her cheeks warming under the intensity of his gaze, and even more disconcerting, felt a thrill of attraction course through her that increased as her gaze met and locked with his.

There was undeniably magnetism about Adam that, despite her self-censure, her femininity was responding to.

'But you have come back, haven't you?' Adam said abruptly, turning his attention to Jodie who, having sniffed noses and been accepted by the other two dogs, was sitting by Lara's side. 'Hello, sweetheart.' The difference in his tone was unmistakeable. He clicked his fingers to the dog and, tail wagging, she came and pushed her nose into the palm of his hand. 'You can always rely on dogs,' he murmured softly, ruffling her thick creamy pelt. 'They never leave you, never let you down.'

'Meaning what exactly?' Lara asked stiffly.

'Exactly what I said.' Adam raised one sardonic eyebrow.

Maria, sensing the undercurrents although baffled as to the reason, intervened diplomatically.

'If we don't eat soon, that casserole will be drying up.'

'Sorry, Gran.'

Adam drew up another chair to the table as she walked away to the kitchenette. Mercurially, he spun round to face Lara.

'Let's forget our first meeting and start again, eh? My gran is a marvellous cook. Is it the first time you've tasted her cooking?'

He was smiling now. Wrong-footed, Lara found herself nodding.

'You're in for a treat.'

There was genuine warmth now in

his eyes. Was he merely being the devoted and courteous grandson, or, as Lara suspected, did he have emotional buttons, raw and hidden perhaps, that she had inadvertently pushed? Whatever, he was an intriguing, complex male, and she was aware of an exciting and dangerous chemistry starting to build between them.

Kate's words came back into her thoughts. Any girl would certainly fancy him on looks alone even without the charisma, both of which he had in quantity. She reminded herself of the reply she'd given Kate. Finding her father came first. If and when she accomplished this, perhaps then might be the time to allow emotional barriers to fall for the right man. But Maria had been generous enough to invite her for a meal and because she had no wish to spoil the evening, Lara returned Adam's olive branch.

'I thought for sure it was baked beans on toast tonight,' she said lightly.

'Sometimes it's not just the food that

matters, but the company.'

'True,' she agreed. 'I'm really looking forward to getting to know Maria.'

'Ouch!'

'Sorry.' Lara bit her lip. 'I really didn't mean it to sound like that.'

'Then I take it you'd also like to get to know me?'

Put on the spot, Lara floundered.

'As Maria's grandson, yes, of course I'd like to. I mean, I expect you often come visiting so we're bound to bump into each other, aren't we?'

'And who knows,' he said, his blue eyes sparkling, 'bumping into each other might even be enjoyable.'

'Oh, good.' Maria came over to the table carrying a laden tray. 'I can see you two are getting on fine.' Adam hastily took it from her. 'Do sit down, Lara,' she urged. 'I'm not into formalities. Good food is meant to be enjoyed whilst it's hot. However, I will just say a short, simple prayer before we begin.' Bending her head she said, 'Knowing our need, we thank you, Father, for the food you have placed before us.'

'It's a long time since I've heard grace said.' Lara took up her knife and fork. 'Grandma Emma always did the honours at home, but it's one of the niceties I left behind.'

'What work do you do?'

Adam regarded her quizzically over the rim of his glass of mineral water.

'I did,' Lara corrected. 'I was in horse racing, in Lambourn.'

'Really?' Adam exchanged a swift glance with Maria. 'That's very interesting.'

'People think it's glamorous. It's not. Hours are long, the work's hard.'

'Hm, back-breaking.'

Lara speared a broccoli floret before slanting a glance at him.

'Are you making fun of me?'

'No, not at all. That is partly the reason I opted out at an early age and decided on journalism instead.'

'What do you mean, opted out? Did you intend working in racing?'

'Since my father's a racehorse trainer,

it was the logical path to take.'

Lara stared in amazement at him.

'Is he really? Whereabouts in the country does he train?'

Maria, who had been sitting silently following the conversation, gave a little choking sound and turned it into a cough. Lara looked across at her, puzzled. Maria's eyes were dancing with merriment.

Adam's expression was deadpan. 'Oh, about half a mile away.'

'About . . . ' Lara wrinkled her brow, thinking furiously. 'You don't mean Pegasus Stables, do you? When I was a youngster, I worked there every week-end. It belonged to Matt. Do you know him?'

'He's my granddad.'

'I don't believe it.' She gaped at him.

'True. He's retired now, though. Dad gave up the stud farm in Surrey and took over the running of Pegasus.'

'Where's Matt living then?'

'Up in Yorkshire, happy as Larry in an old stone farmhouse with views to

'Afters for three?'

'I'm not sure I could manage anything else.' Lara patted her stomach. 'That casserole was one of the best I've tasted.'

'Thank you, my dear. I rarely get a chance to cook for visitors.'

'Come on, Maria, I'm not just a visitor. I'm hoping we'll be good friends.'

'Don't forget me,' Adam said quickly.

'As if I could.'

'Following your theory, do you think we were all meant to meet then?'

Maria chuckled. 'I'll leave you two to grapple with the question whilst I bring the next course. Adam already knows my feelings.'

'Do you, Lara?' Adam persisted.

'Why do I get the impression it's important to you?'

He leaned forward and stared into her eyes. Lara felt her pulses quicken, his gaze was mesmeric.

'Call it destiny, fate, whatever,' she said a little shakily, 'but, yes, yes I do think we have interwoven paths. There are lessons that we can only learn through interaction with other people.'

'No man is an island,' he intoned heavily and she laughed.

Maria caught his words as she placed three glass dishes on the table.

'Whatever you believe, we all need each other.'

'Grandma Emma had you, obviously,' Lara said, 'but did she have any other close friends?'

'Well, I don't know about close, but, yes, she had a small circle of associates.'

'Anyone in particular?'

Maria pondered. 'Henry Jenkins, certainly. Emma used to cook dinner for him about once a fortnight.'

'The solicitor?' Lara's voice reflected her disbelief.

'Yes.'

'Apart from business, I didn't know they met socially. Although, thinking back, he did say he attended Emma's sixty-fifth birthday party.'

Lara dipped a spoon into the

home-made apricot yoghurt topped with butterscotch sauce.

'Mm, this is gorgeous, Maria.'

'Do you know of anybody else, apart from Mr Jenkins that Emma was friendly with?' Lara continued.

'There's old George,' Adam said.

'Of course,' Maria said, 'but you couldn't call him a close friend.'

'I don't see why not,' Adam said, somewhat surprised. 'He often popped round.'

'Who's he?'

'Our local poacher and reprobate.'

'And you're saying this George was a friend of Grandma's?'

'They went back a long way.'

'Really? How long?'

'About the time you were born.'

Lara stared across the table at him.

'Are you talking about George Calledine?'

Adam nodded and Lara went on.

'But he wasn't a reprobate. I knew him when I was a child. He had a wife called Annie, I think.'

'That's right,' Maria said as she poured out coffees.

'He was a farm labourer and they lived in one of the old cottages up at Bracken Farm.'

'Still does,' Adam replied. 'Well, George does.'

'And Annie?'

'She died about three years ago,' Maria said.

'Three years ago today,' Adam murmured. 'I'm glad this came up in conversation otherwise I might have forgotten. I'd thought about George this morning but then work took over.' He glanced at his watch, drained the coffee and stood up. 'I'm afraid I must excuse myself.'

'You're going to the Dog And Duck?'

'Yes, Gran.'

'Don't buy him too many pints.'

'I won't, but he's not going to win his battle now, not at his time of life.'

'Nor does he want to,' Maria said sadly.

Lara looked from one to the other.

'You're talking about meeting George? Emma wasn't his only friend?'

Adam grinned. 'George and I cemented our friendship about the time you started infant school.'

'That presupposes you were around Bingham at an early age.'

'We sometimes came up from Surrey to see Grandad.'

'Do give George my good wishes, won't you?' Maria said.

'Depend on it, Gran.'

'Could I send him mine as well? I'm sure from what you've told me Emma would have been thinking about him. After all, I knew him years ago, too, although I expect he's forgotten all about me.'

'No way, not after what happened.' Adam raised one eyebrow.

'Excuse me?'

'I think it's time you were going, Adam,' Maria said quickly.

'What? Oh, yes, I'd better.'

'Just a minute.' Lara jumped to her feet. 'You can't leave it like that. Tell me what you mean. What did happen?'

'Maria's right, I must push off. George will be down at the pub already. Most nights he gets pretty maudlin but tonight, well . . . '

Adam crossed the room hastily and let himself out.

'Now, why do I feel there's something you both know but don't want me finding out?' Lara asked.

'Remember we were talking about karma? Sooner or later things that happened in the past come around again but until they do, they're best left alone.'

'And I'll have to be satisfied with that?'

Maria grinned. 'I'm sure there will be plenty of other pressing things needing to be seen to.'

Lara, realising she wasn't going to get any further information, said, 'Just promise that you'll tell me when you're ready.'

'My dear, when the time is right, you shall know everything, I promise.'

6

Adam nosed his car out of the yard at Mounts Cottage and headed for his flat above the newspaper office. At this early hour there wouldn't be many at the pub and parking would be easy, but it would be safer to leave the car at home. He'd have to be sociable and have at least a couple of beers.

Bounding up the stairs to the flat, Adam checked his answer-phone for any messages before drawing the curtains. It would be dark by the time he returned and it would make the flat seem a little more homely. Picking up a jacket, he checked keys and cash and went out, dropping the catch.

The pub was only a few minutes' walk away and crossing the market place, he paused and looked back, savouring the quiet peace that enfolded the ancient, cobbled square. A small breeze whispered its way across the square. Beneath his jacket, a cold feeling ran down Adam's spine. This wasn't going to be an enjoyable evening. Of course he could always duck out, leave George to cope alone, but the thought was gone as quickly as it had come.

George hadn't hesitated nor left him, a boy of six, that dreadful day so long ago now. Recalling the evening's conversation with the two women, he considered for a moment if perhaps this was a small karmic payback, then shrugged with a quick dispelling movement and thrust open the pub door.

As expected, the bar was all but empty. Two youngsters sat at a round table in the corner. Totally oblivious to anyone else, they were solemnly sharing a half of bitter. The glass held by both the youth and the girl was being slid to and fro across the polished tabletop without their fingertips parting. Jack felt a pang of envy for their obvious happiness.

A sudden picture of Lara's face floated tantalisingly before him. In your dreams, he admonished himself firmly, banishing the picture.

He sighed, walked over to the bar and asked Gillian, the barmaid, for a pint. Glancing round the near-empty room, he spotted old George slumped in a seat near the window. The poor chap was a lost soul since losing Annie. Adam ordered a further pint, paid for both and went to join the old man.

'Have one on me, George.' He dropped down in the opposite seat. 'I hate drinking by myself.'

George squinted across at him and nodded. 'Ta, lad.'

Adam lowered his beer level and studied him. Usually a free drink would have lit up George's face even if only for a short time, but tonight hopelessness hung over him. He slurped unseeingly at his drink.

'A difficult day for you,' Adam said sympathetically.

After a long silence the old man

raised his eyes, red-rimmed and watery, and focussed blearily on Adam's face.

'Eh, lad, life's a nightmare an' no mistake.'

'There's something else wrong?' Adam asked perceptively.

'Lost 'em both, same day, an' it's hard, lad, real hard.'

'Do you want to tell me? Is there anything I can do?'

The kindness in Adam's voice was more than the old man could bear and his face worked with emotion. He tried valiantly to keep control but two fat tears squeezed themselves from over-flowing eyes.

'Thanks, lad, but there's nought you can do.'

'George, we go back a long way. I've never forgotten what you did for me, what you're still doing for me by keeping silent. Let me help you. Tell me what's happened, please.'

George twisted the glass round and round in horny paws before coming to a decision.

'I blame meself. I should have checked t'back door was closed proper before I set off. Then Gyp couldn't have followed me.'

With prompting, the whole sad tale came out.

'I can't tell you how sorry I am you've lost him,' Adam said and dropped a hand on George's shoulder. 'But look at it this way. Gyp was doing what he wanted, enjoying the freedom to live. He didn't suffer. You know Gyp would have had to be taken to the vet very soon. It's much better this way. If you could ask him, he'd say the same.'

'Aye, lad, maybe you're right. It's just . . . today . . . y'know?'

'I know.' Adam's fingers tightened on the old man's shoulder. 'And there is something I can do for you. Choose the right spot for Gyp and let me do the hard work. Then you can say a proper goodbye and you'll feel better. I'll come round to your cottage tomorrow, but now, I'm going to buy us both another drink.'

He was rewarded by a faint smile.

Back at Maria's, Lara thanked the older woman for the delicious meal and slipped across the yard to Mounts Cottage. She was feeling replete but slightly guilty. For the past hour, Jodie had been giving her meaningful looks. Letting herself in at the kitchen door she lugged in the bags and boxes from her car. Finding a tin opener, she opened up a large tin of dog food.

Lara added a generous amount of mixer and put the bowl on the floor. Whilst the dog had her supper, Lara methodically packed away the food rations and equipment from the cardboard boxes. Then, taking two suitcases upstairs, she dumped them on the landing to be dealt with later.

Rooting in the airing cupboard, she found a matching set of bed linen and walked down the far end to the bedroom overlooking the stables. Dropping the pile of clean sheets on to a chair, Lara went over and sat on the padded window seat looking out at the line of green-painted stable doors. She could still remember the first time she had scrabbled triumphantly on to the wide ledge, pulled herself upright and finally clung on tightly to the window catch. And she also remembered how, looking down at the varnished floorboards so far beneath, she had felt terror grip her.

At the age of two and a half, the only thing to do had been to wail for help. 'Gan! Gan!' The name she had called Grandma Emma came insidiously into her mind. Tears sprang up and blurred the outline of the stable doors. Grandma Emma had come running to the rescue then, holding out loving arms to the frightened child, enfolding, soothing, setting her down safely. Then, taking her hand, she had led the way downstairs and out into the orchard to pick a ripe, juicy apple straight from the tree.

Lara leaned her head against the cold glass of the windowpane.

'Oh, Gan, Gan Emma, I stayed away

too long and now it's too late.'

A warm, wet tongue licked her hand. Jodie had followed her upstairs. Lara brushed away the tears. Life was here, now, and had to be lived, and the dog desperately needed walking. Down in the kitchen, she picked up the lead and took the dog out through the orchard and down the steep bank on to Cuckoo Walk.

Dusk was falling and the air was warm and very still. Lara and Jodie had the walk to themselves. Lara unfastened Jodie's lead and let her run in front. After a day of mostly being confined indoors, the dog rejoiced in the freedom, lolloping along with ground-eating strides. Lara followed at a far more sedate pace, but she found her thoughts roaming as freely as Jodie. And her thoughts were all about the enigmatic Adam. She had the impression that he would have finished what he was telling her had not Maria intervened at the crucial moment. There was no point in speculating what it might be. It could be absolutely anything and as Maria had said, all things came round again in a circle.

She wondered how his evening had gone. Obviously, it would not have been a happy event and she found if difficult to conceive George becoming a reprobate. From what she could remember, he had been a proud, upstanding man. Perhaps his downfall had only begun after Annie's death. Maria had chatted a little after Adam had left the flat, filling her in with some of George's background. She had mentioned he had a dog, a terrier, an old boy called Gyp.

At this moment, Jodie came tearing back down Cuckoo Walk in a burst of mad, released energy, nudged her hand with a wet nose before swirling around and loping away again in front. Her thoughts were arrested as Jodie stopped at a bend of the path and gave a short, warning bark. Lara realised with a twinge of apprehension that dusk had fallen whilst she'd been lost in thought and it was getting really dark. Perhaps it hadn't been such a good idea to go down Cuckoo Walk so late in the evening.

Reaching the bend, she saw a large figure, a man's figure, looming up a few yards away. Dropping a hand, she grasped Jodie's collar, her fingers tightening involuntarily on the rolled leather. But before her apprehension fanned itself into fear, a man's voice broke the silence.

'All right, Lara, it's only me, not the mad axe man.'

Jodie tugged forward, tail wagging as she recognised the man. To have Adam so strongly in her thoughts at that moment, believing him to be down in the pub, only to find him standing on the path in front of her, gave Lara a jolt. It was almost as though by thinking of him she had materialised the man. But as Adam drew level and smiled down at her, she dismissed the silly thought.

'You did surprise me,' Lara admitted. 'I didn't expect to see you on Cuckoo Walk. I thought you were down at the pub with George.'

'I was, well, for part of the evening, but it wasn't quite as bad as I'd feared, although it could very well have been doubly worse.'

'Why?'

'You knew it was the third anniversary of Annie's death?' She nodded. 'Not only that, this morning he lost Gyp.'

'Oh, the poor man,' Lara empathised. 'It's dreadful when you lose your dog.'

They were both silent for a few moments.

'Are you walking any farther?' Adam asked, breaking the silence.

'No. I think Jodie's had enough exercise now and I'm not keen on walking down there on my own, not now it's getting dark.'

'And if I were to offer to come with you?'

She shook her head. Their eyes met and held. There it was again, that unmistakable spark of mutual attraction.

'I'd better get back.'

To hide the effect he was having on her, she bent down and clipped on Jodie's lead.

'May I walk back with you?'

'If you wish, but isn't it out of your way?'

They walked in companionable silence until about halfway back to Mounts Cottage when the sudden spine-tingling hooting of an owl made Lara jump. Instinctively, Adam's hand shot out, cupping her elbow, steadying her.

'It's only an owl. We do get them along here. Plenty of trees, you see.'

'That's something we didn't have when I used to come here as a child.'

'It's rather strange that we have never met before,' Adam mused, keeping in step with her, his hand, Lara noticed, still cupping her elbow.

'Well, there is a difference in age,' she murmured.

'True. But I bet you slid down these banks in winter when it was all snowed up and icy, absolutely glorious. Childhood's pretty special, isn't it?'

'Yes, on both counts,' she agreed.

'And then of course, in the summertime it was just a kid's paradise, wasn't it?' There was an almost wistful note in his voice.

'Sounds like you had a good childhood,' Lara said. 'I certainly did.'

'I did, with perhaps the odd one or two traumas thrown in.'

She looked sideways at him. 'As long as they weren't terrible traumas. A little adversity adds salt to life. Without that we wouldn't appreciate all the other happiness, would we?'

'Oh, I don't know. I think I could have done very well without one or two of mine. Anyway,' he reverted to his normal cheerfulness, 'looks like those are your steps up the bank. Back road into the orchard, yes?'

Lara nodded. 'How did you know that?'

'Don't forget, I was Emma's chief apple-picker. I often slid down those steps afterwards and went home the back way along Cuckoo Walk. Better than the main road, peaceful, no smelly motor cars roaring past. Come on, race you up the steps.'

He won, of course, and they stood panting under the laden fruit trees.

'I'd invite you in for coffee, but I've just moved in tonight, obviously, and I'm not sure where everything is at the moment. It's in a bit of a pickle.'

'I happen to be specially partial to pickle. I'm also partial to hot coffee.'

'Come on then.'

Lara led the way across the stable yard and opened the cottage door. Once inside, Adam headed unerringly for the cupboard containing the instant coffee and the mugs. Lara put her hands on hips.

'You have obviously been in here before,' she said accusingly.

'Of course.' He lifted down a bowl of brown sugar. Then with the air of a magician, dipped farther into the cupboard and produced an ornate tin that Lara recognised instantly. She'd raided it frequently as a youngster. Seeing it again gave her a warm feeling. Truly, home was the very best place.

He executed a bow and placed it on the table.

'Would madam care for a biscuit?'

Lara, laughing, rinsed out and refilled the electric kettle.

They took their drinks through to the cosy lounge and sat in the leather chairs on either side of the open fireplace.

'Pity it's so warm.' Adam inclined his head towards the empty grate that held a tall earthenware jar filled with dried grasses, teasels and bulrushes. 'Nothing like a good crackling fire to make you feel at home instantly.'

Lara, looking across at him, realised it didn't need the ambience of an open fire. Adam already looked as though he belonged here. She slid luxuriously lower in her chair and stretched out her legs, resting them on the edge of the hearth.

'Did you come round to see Gran

apart from your apple-picking stints?'

Busy sipping hot coffee, Adam nodded.

'Often?'

'I popped in when George did, sometimes on my own but mostly with him. We'd often find Mary and Sophie here, too, and Maria, of course.'

'Mary and Sophie?'

'Oh, I keep forgetting. You've only just arrived. Do you know, it's strange but I seem to have known you for much longer, a great deal longer.' He leaned forward, cupping his mug in both hands, eyes gazing at her face. 'And I'd like to get to know you a great deal better, Lara.'

Kate no doubt would have been applauding but Lara parried his unspoken question. Despite his attraction, there was no room in her life right now for either a shallow dalliance nor a serious love affair.

'Firstly, I need to find out as much as I can about my grandma. It's my number one priority. And you haven't told me yet who Mary and Sophie are. Were they close friends of Emma's?'

'Mary Kettlewell was employed by your grandma. Sophie is her daughter, and does some news-gathering for me. She also has a newspaper delivery round.'

Lara stared at him. 'Employed her as what?'

'As cleaner.'

Thinking quickly, Lara said, 'And she's going to be wondering if I'll be keeping her on, yes?'

'Bound to, I guess.'

'The answer will have to be no, I'm sorry, but there's no way I can afford to keep her on. To be frank I haven't got a job myself. I suppose I should make that my first must-do. The trouble is, horses are all I know.'

'You could always study for something else.'

'No. I have to get a job, any job, quickly. I need some money coming in.'

'Is it set in stone you don't want a job with horses?'

'Definitely!' Lara nodded emphatically.

'That's a pity,' he sighed softly. 'If you had been interested, there's a job going here in Bingham. I know it would suit you. One snag, though.'

'There usually is. Still, go on. What job is it?'

'It's a stable job. Actually, a racing stable job. If you took it, you'd be working for my dad, at Pegasus.'

'No!' The word came out sharply.

'Think about it.' He rose to his feet lazily. 'I'd really like to stay longer but it's pretty late.'

Lara glanced at her watch and was amazed to find it well after eleven. He fumbled in his jacket pocket.

'My phone number. Don't dismiss the idea before you've given it some thought. It could tide you over whilst you look around.'

He took her hand.

'Thanks for a very pleasant end to a rough evening.'

'No need to thank me, I enjoyed your company.'

She showed him to the door, switching on the outside light so that he could see his way across the yard. And then, thinking it had sounded rude saying no so abruptly, she called after him, 'Thanks for the job offer, Adam. I will think about it.'

Without turning, he lifted an arm in response before the darkness closed around him and he was gone.

7

Sifting through the mail the following morning, Lara realised she had been high-handed in turning down Adam's offer of a job. The bills were frightening. What was it he had said? Working at Pegasus would tide her over until something else turned up. He was right, it would.

Working in racing, and living at the stables had meant much of the accommodation cost was already found by the trainer. It was a shock to realise, as a property owner, the upkeep and outgoings were considerable. For a start, the amount of monthly council tax on a property the size of Mounts Cottage was like a mini mortgage by itself. Emma's will would undoubtedly have to go through probate and any monies due to her could take months. She was certainly going to have to take the job — choice didn't come into it.

The letterbox rattled and Jodie barked. Lara frowned. The postman had already been so who could it be? She went round to the front to find out. A young girl gripping the handlebars of a bike with one hand was about to rattle the letterbox again. Seeing Lara, she impatiently tossed a single plait of blonde hair out of the way, dipped a hand into a large canvas bag and drew out a newspaper. Deftly folding it, she held out the paper to Lara.

'Do you normally deliver a morning paper?' Lara inquired.

'Uh-huh. After Mrs Denton died, I took it up the steps.' She pointed towards the wooden steps leading to Maria's flat above the stables.

'I see. Mrs Denton was my grandma. My name's Lara. What's yours?'

'Sophie Kettlewell. My mum'll be here this morning as usual, at ten though, instead of nine. Got a dentist's appointment first. Been up half the night she has with toothache.'

'Oh, I'm sorry.

Lara's spirits dropped. The poor woman would be in no state to be told she was no longer wanted.

'How long has she worked for my grandma?'

'Years,' Sophie said cheerfully and straddled the bike, calling back over her shoulder, 'We're both real sorry about your grandma.'

Me, too, Lara thought dispiritedly. She was beginning to realise coming back had presented her with more problems than she'd anticipated. Returning across the yard, Lara saw Maria carefully negotiating the wooden steps.

'Hi. Fancy coming in for a cup of tea? I could certainly do with one.'

'Make it two, then.'

She followed Lara through the kitchen door.

'Sophie brought the paper.' Lara handed it to Maria. 'Did you want to have it or should I?'

'How about we share it and cut the cost?'

'I'm not going to argue. This is the first time I've had a property to look after and to be honest, the outgoings are scary, especially with no income.'

'Are you looking for a job?'

'I must. I can't live on fresh air. Adam's told me there's a vacancy at Pegasus.'

'Working for Jack?'

'Sorry, I keep forgetting he's your son. Is Ellahanta your maiden name?'

'Yes, I reverted after my divorce. So, you're going to take the job, yes?'

'Have to. If I'm offered it, of course.'

'Oh, you'll be offered it all right.'

'You think so?'

The old lady smiled. 'I know so.'

★ ★ ★

At Pegasus racing stables, the little terrier stopped prowling round the long kitchen and went to stand by the back door. Jack Branston, fifty-three last birthday but not showing it, frowned.

'Do you think she's starting?'

'Doubt it. The puppies aren't due for about another week,' his wife, Catherine, replied.

Jack opened the back door. Bettina of Freshington, or Bet, as she was called for short, lumbered out slowly, her body ungainly and cumbersome with the weight of her unborn puppies. Jack closed the door.

'She's OK, she won't go far.'

Catherine nodded without raising her head from the ledger she was poring over.

'I wish two or three owners would hurry up on the payments,' she said. 'We're running pretty tight. The rate we're going, we shall need the income from selling Bet's pups to break even.'

'She's certainly carrying a large litter. With her pedigree, the sale price should balance the books a little. Although, don't forget we've still got to take on another lad. That's more wages to find. You expect it to be rough, Catty, when you're starting up.'

After the death of his first wife, Jack had never expected to find another woman he could love and who would love him. Finding Catherine and her baby son, Adam, had seemed like a rebirth. A weird feeling of déjà vu swept over him and he was back in time twenty-five years ago. Instantly, harshly, he closed his mind against the past. It wasn't something he could allow in. It was far too painful, and it brought back the guilt. He concentrated hard on the present.

'Of course, we could always pack in training horses and take up dog breeding, Catty.'

'No way,' she glowered at him, then realising he was just baiting her, began to laugh.

From outside came the sound of a car driving into the yard followed by several loud barks from Bet. Catherine sighed and closed the ledger.

'I'll go.'

Jack heard her call up the dog before

greeting someone. Moments later she reappeared accompanied by Maria and a young woman.

'Mother,' Jack exclaimed, 'how are you?'

'Well, very well,' Marie returned, 'and this is my friend, Lara.'

Jack turned his full attention on Lara, taking in her high cheek bones, full lips and forget-me-not-blue eyes, all crowned by a rich brown mane of thick hair, at the moment caught back by a heavy slide at the nape of her neck.

'And what do you do? Are you this sorcerer's apprentice?'

Lara, rather irritated by the somewhat mocking tone and his close scrutiny of her, was about to reply when Maria chipped in.

'I suppose you could say so.' She looked from one to the other. 'Why don't you two talk racehorses instead?'

A strange glint came into Jack's eyes.

'Don't tell me you're a horse freak?'

Fully nettled now, Lara retaliated. 'And why shouldn't I be?'

After swallowing the bitter fact she had to return to racing in order to live, it was costing dearly in terms of raw emotion to know whatever happened now, she would never receive her jockey's licence to race. She would have to submerge her deepest desire whilst being continually exposed to seeing other young jockeys achieve their dreams. But it was a pain that had to be endured to stay at Mounts Cottage. Her heart thumping and hands sticky with perspiration, she continued, 'Let me tell you, I rode racehorses at Pegasus years before you came on the scene. And what's more, for the last ten years I've earned my living riding racehorses, maybe not on the tracks, but that's beside the point.'

'And so, you fiery female, why aren't you doing it now?'

All Lara's anger drained away. She shrugged dispiritedly.

'Why indeed.'

She turned to leave. No way would he employ her now, but Jack made a snap decision.

'Be at the stables at seven o'clock tomorrow. You can ride Miss Felham first lot.'

Lara was struck dumb, unable to believe he'd actually given her a trial after her outburst of temper.

'I need someone to ride work. The job's yours, if you want it. 'It will keep you a lot fitter than being a sorcerer's apprentice.'

'How do you know I'm any good?'

'Come off it. You've been in racing ten years. What you have is a serious confidence problem. See you tomorrow, seven o'clock.' Then, walking to the door, he said, 'No rest in racing,' and went off to the stables.

It was after eleven when Lara drove Queen Victoria back into the yard at Mounts Cottage.

'Looks like Mary's here,' Maria said, pointing to an ancient bicycle propped against the kitchen wall.

Lara's relief at being given a paid job, even though it would cost her in other ways, evaporated.

'And I've got to tell her she's redundant.'

'Don't jump fences before you come to them.'

'What do you mean? I can't possibly afford to pay her wages.'

'I think you'll find Mary won't expect you to. Talk to her.'

Reaching for the door latch, Lara was taken by surprise when it opened abruptly and a slim woman in her late thirties with fair hair and lines of tiredness around her blue eyes stood in the doorway. The woman held out her right hand with a smile and said, 'Mary Kettlewell. I was Emma's cleaner. You're Lara Denton, yes?'

Lara was instantly reminded of the young girl with the fair plait of hair.

'That's right. I'm pleased to meet you. How did it go at the dentist?'

'Fine, thanks. One replaced filling and goodbye toothache.'

Minutes later they were sitting at the big kitchen table sipping mugs of coffee. Lara looked at the long, gleaming run of floor.

'You've made a smashing job of the tiles.'

'It's said you can tell a woman's character from the kitchen and bathroom. Mrs Denton was very particular about the tiles.'

Lara suddenly pictured her grandma wagging an admonishing finger at her and saying, 'When will you learn, Lara, boots are left outside in the porch.' She smiled at Mary. 'Yes, I know she was.'

'I was fond of her, you know.' Mary shook her head sadly. 'It was a shock to hear in the shop that she'd been rushed into hospital. Why, I'd only been talking to her a couple of days before. Right as rain she was then. I was going to visit her, take her some flowers, but it was all so quick.'

'How long was she in? Nobody has told me anything. I didn't even know she'd taken ill, you see.'

Mary shook her fair curls and clucked with annoyance.

'Only in a day, she was, died that same night. A stroke, they say.'

'Yes,' Lara said slowly, 'the solicitor told me it was a stroke.'

'I suppose if you've high blood pressure you're more prone to them, although I've always thought it took some upset to trigger them off.'

'And did my grandma have any upset, do you know?'

'She had two visitors the day it happened apparently.'

'Two?' Lara frowned.

'The last time I saw Mrs Denton it should have been bedroom-cleaning day. Anyway, she asked me to skip them and give the dining-room a good going over. Oh, and the downstairs cloakroom and toilet, fresh soap and towel, too, just in case he needed to go.'

'Who?'

Mary looked surprised. 'Why Mr Jenkins, of course.'

'The solicitor?'

'Well, yes, he is a solicitor.'

'But he didn't come in his official capacity?'

'Gracious, no. I thought you'd have known, like.'

'I've been away ten years. I was barely sixteen when Grandma banished me from Mounts Cottage because I went into racing as a career. I have no idea of her life, or her friends. I didn't even know about Maria, or yourself.'

'Oh, I see.'

'Do you know who the second caller was that day?'

'I really couldn't say. Perhaps Maria knows.'

'Look Mary, I have to be straight with you. I can't afford to employ a cleaner . . . '

'Please,' Mary interrupted, 'before you say anything, I was going to tell you. I can't come any more, not to clean. For a long time now I've been preparing to start afresh, do something I want to do. Sophie's thirteen now, not a baby anymore and that frees me to think about my future. Next weekend, I'm going away on a short course for beginners learning reflexology. That's only the start, of course. Afterwards I've a place booked at South Notts College.'

'Good for you. But what about Sophie? How will she cope?'

'It's worrying me no end. You see, Maria very kindly said Sophie could stay with her. Maria's lovely but she's . . . she's . . . '

'An old lady?'

'Yes. You see what I mean. You can understand why I'm concerned. I do need to attend this course but I'm torn about leaving her.'

'Then don't be.' Lara smiled. 'I'd be happy to keep an eye on both of them. You looked after Grandma very well. Let me return the favour.'

'Really? It would be such a relief.'

'Settled, then. And you don't know what a relief it is to me that you don't want the job. I was dreading telling you.'

'I'd told Sophie not to mention it to

anyone before I told you myself.'

'I wonder how Maria knew.'

'Did she?'

'Seemed to.'

Mary giggled. 'Well, she is clairvoyant.'

'Anyway, I met Sophie delivering the newspaper this morning but she didn't tell me.'

'She's dead-set on becoming a journalist. Maria's grandson, Adam, that is, Mr Branston, he's our local newspaperman and she helps him out a bit. He's such a kind person. Have you met him yet?'

'Yes, Adam came in for a coffee last night.'

'Mrs Denton often had him and George here for a drink and a chat. They'll both miss her.'

'I'd like to meet George again. I used to know him when I was a child. Still, I shouldn't think he's on the phone.'

'No, I'm sure he's not. But Sophie could always ask Mr Branston to have a word with him.'

'Thanks, I'd like that. I'm trying to build up a picture of Grandma's life since I've been away.'

'She always kept a diary, I know that. Many a time I've arrived for work and found her scribbling away. It was a large thick one, with a dark-blue cover and a lock.'

Lara felt a rush of excitement. 'Do you know where she kept it?'

'In the bureau as far as I know. Is it important, then?'

'Maybe.' Lara hesitated. Mary was a stranger, but she'd proved trustworthy with Emma. 'What I'm really trying to do, Mary, is trace my natural father.'

'Oh. Sounds like you need to find your birth certificate.'

'I have a short version but it doesn't give all the details a full one would.'

'Have you applied to the Superintendent Registrar at West Bridgford?'

'To be honest, I've not had time. I only decided to try and find my father after I heard Grandma had died.'

Mary's eyes shone with excitement.

'Do you think it could be a local man? Just imagine, if you actually find him it would be marvellous.'

'Always assuming he wants me to.'

'Why wouldn't he?'

Lara shook her head. 'He's never looked for me, has he?'

'Perhaps he didn't know where to look.'

'I don't know where to look either. But it's not going to stop me trying.'

8

Lara, over-riding her immediate impulse to search for Emma's diary after Mary left, decided to leave it until later when she had the necessary time. After a hasty lunch of crackers and cheese, she'd taken Jodie for a much-needed walk. Now, coming back through the orchard, she could see the familiar black saloon parked in the yard.

Her pulses quickened as she saw Adam climb out. Dressed casually in black jeans and white short-sleeved shirt, somehow he still managed to look smart. He was certainly a very handsome man. She suddenly, desperately, wished she wasn't wearing her old jogging bottoms and baggy top. It was too late now, of course. He spotted her and waved.

'Hi, Lara. Looks like we've both timed it right.'

'Doesn't it.' She quickened her pace and drew level. Casting a quick glance at the car, she saw a man sitting in the passenger seat.

'Let me introduce George.'

Adam held open the door and the elderly man clambered out. Lara took in the shabby but clean cords and the unmistakably old yet fresh shirt and felt a stab of pity combined with sadness. He had obviously taken trouble to smarten himself up ready to meet her.

'Hello, George. It's been such a long time since we've met.'

'I'm right pleased to see you again, Miss Lara.'

He eagerly held out a work-roughed hand and gripped hers.

'Sophie dropped by the office at lunchtime,' Adam said. 'She told me you were keen to meet George, so, here we are.'

'I'm so glad you did. Please, come on in.'

Pretending not to notice the eager way George was fondling Jodie's head, she led the way into the cottage.

'Cold beer suit you two chaps?'

'That'd be champion, lass.'

George rubbed his hands. They were sitting in the wing chairs putting all to rights when she carried through the tray of cold drinks. Adam immediately leaped up and took it from her.

'You've altered since I last clapped eyes on you,' George said, a roguish twinkle lurking in his eyes.

Lara, glad to see him cheerful, nodded.

'I'm catching you up in age now.'

'You're the spit of your mam, bless her.'

'Really?' Lara sipped her chilled lime juice and tried to contain her delight that the subject driving her had come up. She'd hoped George might be able to fill in details of her grandma's life but to realise that he had actually known her mother was a wonderful bonus. 'Tell me all about her.'

She leaned forward.

An hour later, Adam, having brought

in necessary refills, was sharing the settee with her now, their drinks on the long coffee table in front. He sat silent, listening to George recounting memories from years past.

'Y'see, lass, working for your grandad part-time when he was busy, I knew your mam when she was nobbut a nipper. A rare temper she had an' all, even at that young age.' He chuckled and shook his head.

'Do you suppose it might have been passed on?' Adam murmured trying to keep a straight face and failing.

'Ignore him, George. You carry on, it's absolutely fascinating.'

'Aye, a real little daredevil she was as a youngster. Come to think about it, right up to the end of her life she lived at full pelt.'

'Tell me, how did she die?'

It was Adam's turn now. He clasped both hands between his knees and looked across at the old man.

'A tragedy, that's what it was. So full of life, Esther was. She'd saddled Oliver and gone off for a ride.'

'But, George, she was expecting me, wasn't she? It was a dreadful risk.'

'Oh, aye. But when she got an idea in her head nothing could stop her. An' there's something else.' He pursed his lips and mused a moment. 'I've never mentioned it to anyone else but she'd had an argument and was in a rare old temper.'

Lara felt a finger of apprehension run down her spine.

'Who did she quarrel with?' she whispered.

George drained the last of his second cold beer.

'I wish it could be different but you need facts, don't you, lass?'

She nodded, her eyes never leaving his face.

'On the day she died, Esther had a fight with Emma.'

'I thought you were going to say that.' Lara's face had gone very white. 'What did they fight about? Do you know?'

'Aye. Emma told me, afterwards, a long time afterwards.'

'Please, George, don't try and spare me, I must know.'

Adam slipped an arm around her shoulders and pressed her close. She was aware of his warmth and strength supporting her. It felt good.

'Emma blamed herself for what happened that day. Y'see, she demanded that Esther told her who the father was.'

'And my mother refused,' Lara said flatly.

'Aye, lass, she did. Swore she'd take his name to the grave.'

There was a heavy silence.

Finally, Adam said, 'And she died that day?'

'The stallion bolted with her. It was wicked bad luck that there was a tanker train coming and the horse got on to the line . . .'

Adam's fingers dug hard into Lara's shoulder.

'Carry on, George, please. Tell me all of it.'

'Esther was tossed off by the impact. She landed the other side of the track, on ploughed land. Oliver was killed instantly. But Esther, she was still conscious when I reached her.'

'What?' Lara gasped. 'You found my mother?'

'I did.'

'I never knew that. Emma never told me.' Lara's anguished voice tailed away and, shivering uncontrollably, she leaned against Adam's comforting shoulder. 'You said she was still conscious. Did she . . . did my mother say anything to you?'

He squared back his shoulders and whispered, 'She did.'

Lara's fingers gripped the arm of the settee, knuckles showing white.

'Did she tell you who my father is?'

'Yes, lass, Esther entrusted me with your father's name.'

'I can't believe it,' Lara said, her voice filled with disbelief.

★ ★ ★

Lara and Adam were having dinner. Adam had arrived at seven. Brushing aside her protests that she wasn't in the mood to go out, even less to eat, he'd insisted it was what she needed. He'd driven out down winding lanes to an old country pub sitting on the banks of the Grantham canal. It had an air of peace and tranquillity about it with the water lapping lazily by and the only sign of life, a small flotilla of mallards.

Inside, however, the pub was filled with people. Adam steered her to a quiet table by the window. When the meal arrived, Lara suddenly realised she was actually very hungry. Adam cast a swift glance at her, smiled to himself and refrained from talking, allowing her space to enjoy the food.

For a few minutes they ate in appreciative silence. Then Lara put down her fork and said, 'George is the only person who knows who my father is, and he won't tell me. I can't believe it. He's your friend, Adam. Couldn't you persuade him?'

'He's acting in what he thinks is the right way.'

'But it's vitally important to me. Can't you see that?'

'I can, yes, and I suppose George must do but don't forget, he made a solemn promise to your mother on her death-bed.'

'And if extreme circumstances made it necessary, he could be released from that promise and divulge my father's name.'

'Lara, it isn't me who must decide, it's George.'

'And you're on his side?' Anger flared in her eyes.

Floundering, he shook his head.

'I'm not on either side, but I can't help feeling responsible for your distress. It's my fault. I shouldn't have asked George how your mother died. It wasn't my business. It was stupid of me.'

'No,' she sighed, 'no, it wasn't. It was perfectly natural. You didn't have any idea just how horrific the situation was.'

'I do now.' His fingers tightened around hers. Their eyes met and held as he said huskily, 'I really wish we could have met under different circumstances, Lara.'

'So do I,' she gulped, shaken to realise just how much she wanted this man in her life.

'Do you think, if only for this evening, we could forget about what happened earlier today? Allow ourselves to enjoy what we have?'

'What do we have, Adam?'

'You already know. We have the one thing we need, that vital spark. Don't say you aren't aware of it.'

And she couldn't deny it. The attraction between them had been there right from the start.

'I made myself a promise,' she said, 'that finding my father was my first priority. OK, I've had to amend it to second place because I desperately needed to get a job.'

He raised an eyebrow in mute query.

'Yes, and yes, is the answer to that. I

went up to Pegasus to see about the job you mentioned.'

'And the second yes, was it that my father offered you a start?'

She nodded. 'Tomorrow morning, seven o'clock.'

'Seriously, how do you feel about returning to racing?'

'Ask me after morning shift. Honestly, I'm so wrecked by this afternoon's talk, it hasn't registered yet.'

'Let's take our coffee out and sit by the water. Give yourself a breather from all the stress.'

Adam leaned forward and looked into her eyes. There was a caring warmth in his gaze that Lara found wonderfully soothing and supportive. He was like no other man she'd ever met.

Later, his arms encircled her as they sat together on the settee after they'd returned to Mounts Cottage. She could feel his warm breath on her cheek and smell the faint fresh tang of his aftershave. Before she could answer, his lips brushed hers in tender butterfly kisses. She slid her arms around his neck feeling the thick hair curling between her fingertips. He drew his lips away a little.

'I've been wanting to kiss you all evening,' he said thickly.

A low whine from Jodie finally impinged into their private world.

'Duty's calling,' Lara whispered.

'I know.' Adam sighed as with deep regret, he rose to his feet. He cupped her cheeks in both hands and slowly kissed her once more.

9

Lara drove into the yard at Pegasus stables and parked at the side of the tack-room. Just for a moment she allowed herself to sit and savour the sight and feel of being back in a stable yard at early morning. Inclining her head at Jodie who dropped her ears but obediently lay down on the old rug in the back of the car, Lara climbed out, breathed in the deeply satisfying smell of stables and warm horses, and went in search of Jack. He wasn't hard to find. Pulling his weight, literally, with the rest of the stable lads, he appeared from the tack-room with a hand trailer loaded with feed buckets.

'You made it then. Welcome aboard! You can muck in with the rest regarding feeding and then tack up Miss Felham.'

'Makes a change, being told to muck in instead of muck out.'

'That comes later.'

Despite Lara's misgivings about taking the job, she had to admit she liked this man. He introduced her to the stable lads, Joey and Craig, then left her to integrate into the feeding and watering stable routine. Being Sunday, she was the only one riding out today.

Lara picked up some tack and went into Miss Felham's stable.

'I could take you over some fences, girl.'

Lara ran a hand down her neck and smoothed the hair down over the mare's withers. Cupping her palm over the velvet muzzle, she teased open the mare's jaw and slipped the bit in over her tongue before drawing the bridle over her head. Miss Felham whickered softly as Lara put on the saddle and drew up the girth. She led the mare out into the stable yard.

Jack came up on the mare's nearside, cupped his hands for Lara's left knee and boosted her into the saddle. Circling Miss Felham, Lara waited for

Jack to mount then followed his horse, trotting out of the yard up the field on to the gallops. Squeezing her calves against the mare's sleek sides, she thrilled as the animal moved smoothly into a canter. The turf flashed past beneath them and she pushed her into a gallop. The big mare responded eagerly, long strides swallowing ground effortlessly.

Lara leaned forward over the thick mane, urging her on. Exhilaration at being astride a racehorse was made all the sweeter after the bitterness of believing she would never ride one again. They reined in at the end of the gallops and Lara bent forward, slapping Miss Felham's firm neck.

'That was great,' she whispered, joy coursing through her.

The mare flicked one ear back to catch the sound, snorted and flexed her neck. Already, Lara admitted to herself, her calves and thighs ached and the unfamiliar saddle had rubbed the inside of her knees, but inside she felt only deep joy at doing what she had always wanted.

'You certainly proved me right.' Jack trotted his horse upsides. 'It's not skill you're lacking, just confidence in your own ability.'

'Does that mean I've a permanent job?'

'Of course. Now let's get breakfast. Catty wants you to have it with us.'

Bet, from her basket, gave a token woof as they entered the kitchen.

'It'll be interesting to see how many puppies she has.'

Lara leaned over and stroked the dog's head before following Jack's lead and washing hands at the sink.

'Fried egg sandwich be OK?'

'Sounds wonderful.'

Catherine had just cracked eggs into the frying pan when the kitchen door swung open and Adam appeared.

'Smelled breakfast?' Catherine said as she spooned hot fat over the eggs.

'Well, if there's any going spare . . . '

She reached for the remaining two.

Adam turned to Lara. 'How'd it go on the gallops?'

'Exactly as I expected it to,' Jack interrupted. 'She's a natural.'

'Unlike me.'

'I haven't thanked you properly for telling me about the job.'

Lara knew by the warm glow that her cheeks had turned pink at the sight of him but was powerless to stop the blush. Adam's presence alone was enough to send sparks fizzing through her. Catherine, however, was deftly sliding eggs from the pan on to slices of wholemeal bread. Lara gratefully took the plate offered and bent her head over it.

'Hm, you are the world's best mother at cooking eggs. Did you know that?' Adam said.

'Just for the flattery, how would you like to share Sunday dinner?' Catherine turned to Lara. 'Are you free this evening? We eat around seven. Please say yes. It will square up the numbers.'

'I'd love to, if you're sure.' Lara

looked at Jack uncertainly.

'We're sure,' he said.

The evening was a delight, made more so by Adam's presence. She had, however, firmly turned down his eager offer to see her home. Although in her heart, Lara already knew he was the one, their relationship needed to slow down a little whilst they both seriously thought about where it was inevitably heading. They agreed to meet at the pub on Wednesday evening.

Her life suddenly seemed to be right on track. The one missing piece of the jigsaw was still not knowing her father's name.

Now, turning the key to let herself in at Mounts Cottage, Lara felt a surge of excitement at the thought that Emma's diary might contain the answer. Jodie, delighted at having her back, trotted after her into the room Emma had used as a study. The solid oak bureau stood waiting. Unlocking it with the key taken from behind the wall mirror, she rolled back the lid. Inside, the pigeon holes were filled with receipts and old letters. Ignoring them, she opened the drawer beneath and drew out a dark blue notebook. The tiny key was still in the brass lock.

Taking it through to the sitting-room, she switched on the standard lamp and sank into one of the wing chairs. An hour later she was still immersed in the fascinating daily accounts of Emma's life when a knock sounded on the door and Jodie barked.

'It's me, Maria. May I come in?'

''Course, I'm in the sitting-room.'

'I know it's getting late but I saw your light on.'

'Is anything wrong?'

'Not wrong, no, but I've been wrestling with my conscience and it won.'

'Did it?' Lara frowned.

'Indeed it did,' Maria replied and held out a carved, oak box.

'Why, that holds our family Bible.'

'Yes. I took it over to the flat when Emma was rushed to hospital.'

Lara sat very still. The old lady's hands were trembling a little.

'Were you trying to protect me?' she asked intuitively.

'Yes. But I've decided you need to know the truth, well, as much as I know.'

Could it be George wasn't the only one who knew her father's name? Slowly, heart pounding, Lara stood up.

'Are you trying to tell me you know who my father is?'

Maria shook her head sadly. 'That I don't know, my dear.'

The disappointment was sharp.

'Inside are four certificates.'

She put the box down on the table, lifted out the Bible and revealed the official documents in the hollow beneath. The top one was a standard birth certificate which gave Emma's date of birth and both parents' names. Next was Emma's marriage certificate, stating her husband's name and the date of their marriage. She'd been eighteen.

Lara lifted out the third certificate. It was her mother's, Esther's, birth certificate, also a standard version, giving the date of birth, a year earlier, but simply naming the mother. In the space reserved for the father's name was a row of small dashes. She lifted her gaze and stared at Maria.

'So, not only was my mother some man's mistress, my grandma was, too. Well, this is where the pattern ends,' Lara said harshly, fighting back tears, 'I'm certainly not following their example.'

She snatched up the last birth certificate, her own, and scanned it quickly. All the details were correct, but in the space reserved for the father's name was also a row of small dashes.

Despairingly, tears now escaping from flooded eyes, she said, 'Oh, Maria, what am I to do? Every opening seems a dead end.'

'I don't know, Lara, and I certainly don't want to raise your hopes, but Emma wanted me to give you some letters. She wrote them but never posted any. They are already in the bureau.'

'Why didn't she post them to me?'

'I don't know. Why do any of us do illogical things? But she loved you very much, I do know that. And she missed you . . . ' Maria broke off, fumbling for a tissue and wiping her eyes. 'I'm off home now. You need time on your own.'

'You're a good friend, Maria, and a brave one. Thank you.'

She held out her arms and they hugged tightly.

When she'd left, Lara made some strong coffee before flicking through the bureau contents. The letters took no finding. They were caught together with an elastic band. She read them in date order. Then sat staring at the opposite wall whilst silent tears flowed down her cheeks for all the lost time that could never be regained, and the coffee remained untouched.

10

Adam glanced away from his computer screen and looked at his watch. The digital read three-fourteen. Any second now, the kids from the comprehensive up the lane would be coming out. Maybe Sophie would turn up. Any piece of news, gossip or information of any sort she heard about was relayed at the double.

He hadn't asked Lara how Mary had taken the news she'd lost her job. He must remember to ask her tonight when they met. It had seemed an eternity waiting for Wednesday, but it certainly proved how much he'd missed her. After Julie's betrayal, he'd been too wary of getting hurt to date anyone, but Lara was different. She wasn't just anyone. She was the one.

Sophie walked straight in and hitched herself on to the edge of his desk.

'What's new then, Sophie, girl?'

'Miss Baston, y'know, the teacher at school? She went crazy at us this afternoon. Me and Debbie had to try not to giggle. Real funny it was. Not for Miss Baston, of course,' she added hastily, 'but it was for the rest of us.'

'Go on then.'

'Peeling a banana, she was, and the skin fell on to the tiles. Well, she stepped back to see where it was, put one foot on it and ended up flat on her back with both legs in the air.'

'You kids,' he shook his head. 'Did she hurt herself then?'

'Yes, she did. The ambulance came right up to the school entrance. She's gone to the Queen's for an X-ray on her ankle. Could be broken.'

'Let's hope not.'

'Can you use it, y'know, in the paper?'

'Sure,' he replied and flipped two coins over the desk to her. 'That it?'

' 'Cept for my own news.'

'And what's that?'

'Mum's going away on a course. I'm staying with your gran.'

'What sort of course?'

'Reflexology. She's going to South Notts College as well, afterwards. No more cleaning for her, she says. Doing her own thing, she is.'

'I'm pleased for her. Wish her luck from me, won't you?'

'Sure. Will I see you when I'm at Maria's?'

Cautiously, he said, 'Might do.' He was desperately hoping Lara would take the brake off their relationship so he could visit her at Mounts Cottage.

Sneaking a quick look at his watch, Adam saw it was just four o'clock, not long now. In just three hours he'd know if it was all on-going between them.

George was sitting at his usual table in the pub when Adam walked in. Going up to the bar, Adam nodded enquiringly across towards the almost empty glass and George lifted an index finger and nodded back.

'Cheers, George.' Adam set down

two foaming glasses.

'Ta, lad.'

'You're looking a bit down. What's the matter?'

'I've summat to tell 'ee, lad, an' you're not going to like it.'

'Hey, what have I done?'

'I've seen Jack.'

'So?'

'He tells me you're getting friendly with Emma's granddaughter.'

'And what's wrong with that?'

The old man looked distressed.

'Because you and me don't have secrets, we help each other out, and because there's something you should know about Lara, lad.'

'If it's bothering you that much, you'd better get it off your chest.'

So George told him.

Adam's smile faded, and the shock took all the colour from his face, leaving him deathly pale.

'No way! You can't be serious. George, tell me you're just winding me up.' But even as he said it, Adam knew from the look on George's face that the old man meant every word.

'You think I'd make up something like that? Nay, lad.'

Adam jumped up, knocking the table and slopping beer.

'You should have told me before,' he cried, utterly devastated. 'You let me get to know her, fall in . . . ' He slammed a fist down on the table. 'Five minutes! Five minutes, and she'll be here. You'd better tell her why I've gone, George, because, so help me, I can't face her.'

He turned and rushed out of the pub and a few minutes later Lara walked in. She spotted George and immediately ordered him a pint along with her white wine spritzer.

'Good to see you, George. How're you doing?'

She sat down beside him.

'Could be better,' he mumbled.

'Oh? What's wrong?'

'They say a little knowledge is a bad thing, and happen they're right.'

'You've lost me. Have you seen any sign of Adam? I'm supposed to be meeting him here.'

George sighed deeply. This was going to hurt him every bit as much as it would hurt her.

'Yes, I've seen him. He's been, and gone. Looked at the clock, saw it was five to seven and skiddadled so's he wouldn't have to meet you.'

Lara stared at him. 'Why on earth did he do that?'

'Told me to tell you, he can't face you.'

'I see.'

Lara bent over her drink. Disappointment flooded every cell in her body. He had obviously used their time apart to think and had reconsidered their relationship. Lara pushed her glass away and stood up.

'Got to go, George. See you.'

She didn't break down. Jodie greeted her effusively and Lara made herself a strong black coffee. Men were bad news. Who needed them, especially when they had a dog to rely upon? The most positive thing that had come from their short relationship was the fact she now had a job and an income that would support her living at Mounts Cottage.

To keep her mind occupied, she began to systematically go through the papers in the bureau. Amongst all the material that had accumulated over years were several very interesting items. Not least was a very old love letter addressed to Emma. It was obviously written with tender, deeply-felt emotion and referred to their exquisite secret time together in, of all places, the old hayloft above the tack-room. Maria's flat now, Lara thought. Whoever had written it, had undoubtedly been in love with Emma.

A sudden thrill of joyous excitement ran through her as she realised that this man must have been Esther's father, and, therefore, he was her natural grandad. Inadvertently, she'd discovered another piece of the jigsaw.

Eagerly she turned the page to read the signature. The letter was signed simply, **Teddy bear**. Frustration surged through her. Who on earth was Teddy bear? Turning the letter over, she saw there was no address, only a phone number written above the date. Would it be possible to cross refer it with today's six digits?

Leaving that to puzzle over later, Lara read on. Teddy bear was obviously very young. He referred to sitting his exams and went on to say his parents were sending him abroad travelling for a year before he began studying in earnest. The telephone number was the only one Emma could contact him on for the following week. To ring at home would be a disaster if his parents answered . . . But what was a year, when he'd love her for ever?

Lara put the letter down. Could this man still be alive? If so, she had gained a grandad she'd never known about. Emma's husband had always been grandad to her until his death years ago. Now, unexpectedly, she had another blood relation, if she could trace him.

She picked up Emma's death certificate that Maria had placed in the bureau. Again, surprise gripped her. Emma had indeed suffered a stroke but the words aortic aneurysm were given first. Lara frowned. It was neither a visitor nor an upset that had brought about Emma's death. The stroke had followed the aneurysm. The next item was a large manilla envelope. Inside was a draft will and a letter from the solicitors. The will was identical to the one she'd already seen. She was about to file it when she noticed something written at the top of the solicitor's letter, and Mr H. R. Jenkins, the senior partner had signed it.

For a long time Lara sat and pondered. She could see most of the picture forming before her but there were three or four pieces still missing. The answers to these she knew were here in Bingham. But the main question was how to uncover them. Several people knew just one of the pieces, but none knew them all.

And then she read the letter Emma had left for her with the solicitors. It had remained in her shoulder-bag unopened until now. Choked with emotion, as she was by Emma's words, it answered that all-important main question.

The solution now presented itself with crystal clarity.

Lara saw exactly how she could discover the vital pieces. All it would take on her part was the nerve to set it up. And suddenly, she was terrified, not only of putting it into action, but also of what the answers might be.

11

On Friday evening, Lara had just returned from work and thankfully kicked off her jodhpur boots when there was a knock at the back door. Mary Kettlewell and Sophie stood outside. Sophie was toting a large holdall.

'I thought we'd pop in before we go to Maria's,' Mary said. 'Let you know it's still on-going this weekend.'

'Glad you did.' Lara smiled at them. 'Fancy a quick coffee?'

'Do I?' Mary rolled her eyes. 'I've been dashing about all day. A boost of caffeine would be lovely.'

'Me, too. You and Adam had a row, then?'

Lara gasped. 'What is this? Have you caught Maria's gift?'

'Now then, our Sophie, don't be so rude.' Mary frowned.

'Nothing's secret in Bingham,' Sophie said cheerfully.

'Seems like it.'

'He's dead upset. Had a row with his dad, too, according to George.'

'Talking about the Branstons reminds me,' Mary said, accepting her coffee gratefully. 'You were asking me the other day about who the second visitor was the day your gran fell ill.'

'That's right, I did.' Lara was thankful the conversation had moved away from the delicate subject of Adam. She hadn't broken down on Wednesday evening after talking to George at the pub but she'd sobbed herself to sleep last night. She'd been thankful when the alarm clock rang at five-thirty this morning and she could get up, start the day and leave her disturbing dreams behind.

But she had to face him tomorrow. She didn't know how, but it had to be done. She could have been honest and said straight out she'd be seeing him, but a large part of the plan was the surprise element. Each of the five people she'd invited for a drink on Saturday evening knew nothing whatsoever about the other four. A successful outcome would depend on catching them all unawares and the degree of open-heartedness they felt when confronted by one another.

'Oh, yeah,' Sophie said, 'it was Jack Branston. Saw him going in when I was on my way to school.'

'Right,' Lara said thoughtfully, 'thanks for the information.'

'Is it important?'

'All the little bits make a picture. It's not complete but I'm working on it.'

When Mary and Sophie left, Lara poured a second coffee and went into the study. Opening the bureau she took out a letter. It was the one Emma had asked the solicitor to give her. At the time Lara had slipped it into her shoulder bag and forgotten about it until late on Wednesday night. Reading all the other letters had jogged her memory and she'd taken it from her bag and read it.

If you are reading this, Lara, I know you are coming home to Mounts Cottage and I hope you will stay. That for me is enough. I shall rest peacefully knowing we are united. Maybe not on the earth plane in the physical body but in all the other aspects that really matter. As you will no doubt discover, there are secrets that need to be revealed, some of these are old, long-standing secrets. It is time for the truth to be told.

I cannot help you, my darling Lara, because I do not know, except to say, the answers all lie here in Bingham. The key people, if you have not already found out are Maria, George, Jack and Adam Branston and my solicitor, Mr Henry Jenkins. Together they hold the keys. Ask them to tell you their secret. This is my last request of each of them, my dear, dear friends, that they tell you their individual secret. Then it is up to you to fit the pieces together. May your finished picture be beautiful, I love you.

God bless you all, Emma.

Lara sighed deeply and folded the single page. Tomorrow evening would be the time to take it from the bureau and read Emma's words out loud to all the assembled guests. Everyone, with the exception of George, had accepted the invitation. He'd protested, saying it wasn't his kind of thing. Lara had regretfully given up and let the subject drop when George started to get upset. The last thing she wanted was to antagonise him. There was always the hope that he would change his mind at the last minute and turn up. The others were all on a promise to come at seven o'clock.

Her stomach churned just thinking about it. How on earth she would cope she honestly didn't know, but there was still tomorrow to get through first and she was due in at the stables at six.

By nine-thirty next morning, she'd ridden out on first and second lots and had just finished breakfast when Catherine came over to the lads' quarters.

'When you've finished eating, Lara, could you pop over to the kitchen?'

'No problem. I've just finished.'

She followed her across the yard and caught her up at the kitchen door. The older woman took her arm.

'Look,' she whispered, 'it's all happening.'

And it was. In a whelping box in a corner of the room, Bet was straining in the last throes of giving birth. Moments later there was a tiny sound.

'Puppy number two,' Catherine said proudly.

'Any idea how many more?'

'Quite a few by the size of Bet. It could be well on in the day by the time the last one's born. I'm desperately hoping there aren't any complications.'

'I'd love to see them all.'

'I'll let you know.'

'You sound as proud as if you'd given birth yourself. But does this mean you can't make it for drinks this evening?'

She had asked both Jack and

Catherine. Jack's presence was essential but she'd invited Catherine out of politeness.

'Sorry,' Catherine said regretfully, 'I really can't leave her. But Jack's still coming.'

Lara heaved an inward sigh of relief. Everything depended on this evening. If it was a success, by the time she went to bed tonight, she'd have gained both a father and grandfather.

Returning home after morning stables, Lara made herself an omelette for lunch and took Jodie for a walk.

'It'll have to be a quick one,' she told the dog.

There was still lots to do, trays of glasses to be set out, bottles to be arranged, crisps and peanuts, still in their packets, to be put into dishes ready to be ripped open and poured in at the last moment to ensure their freshness. And she simply must catch at least an hour's sleep before going back to do evening stables.

But after work, it was amazing what a

hot bath followed by a complete make-up could do. By the time it was a quarter to seven, she was ready. Dressed in a cowl-necked dress in palest lilac and high-heeled sandals, with her hair pinned up, she looked very sophisticated. For the finishing touch, she was just spraying on perfume when the first person arrived. Her stomach knotted into a tight ball and for a moment she felt quite squeamish. Before she could reach the door, it opened and Sophie popped her head round.

'I did knock.'

Lara's tension vanished. She laughed and gave the girl a quick hug.

'What can I do for you?'

'Could I take Jodie for a walk? I promise I won't be gone long.'

'You're an angel. She's hardly had any exercise today and I've a houseful of guests due.'

'I know. Maria's on her way now.' Sophie inclined her head as Maria came in through the open door. 'Right,

I'm off with the dog, then.'

Whistling to Jodie, Sophie took the leash and disappeared.

'You're looking lovely, my dear,' Maria said and kissed Lara's cheek.

'Thanks for the confidence boost, but I don't feel lovely inside. I'm scared stiff.'

'Don't forget, everyone coming tonight will be feeling the same.'

Lara stared at her. 'Do you think so?'

'Exposing secrets, long-held and deeply-buried secrets, will be traumatic for each of them.'

A knock sounded on the door. Lara took a deep breath.

'Here we go.'

It was Henry Jenkins, dressed for once very informally.

'Lara, thank you for inviting me, my dear.'

'I'm glad you could come.'

'Are there to be many of us?'

'Only four, and myself. George couldn't come.'

He looked at her shrewdly. 'Let me

guess. Jack and Adam Branston still to arrive?'

'That's very perceptive of you.'

There was a further knock on the door.

'Please excuse me.'

She went to open it. On the doorstep stood Jack and Adam.

'Hope we're not late,' Jack said.

'No, not at all, come in.'

Her eyes met Adam's. She was appalled. For the briefest of moments, the naked suffering was transparently clear before a veil dropped and they were hard, impersonal. But that tiny glimpse into his innermost feelings had been enough. Ignoring the cold look, hope flared within her. Beneath the make-up and the self-control, Lara's personal agony had seen itself reflected in Adam's eyes. His face, too, gave away how he felt.

He had been curt to the point of rudeness on the telephone when she rang a couple of days ago to invite him over. It was only when she'd stressed it was imperative he should be there that he'd most reluctantly agreed. She showed them through to the sitting-room.

Maria had already helped herself and Henry Jenkins to a drink and Lara hastened to pour one each for Jack and Adam. Taking her own, she gripped the glass tightly to stop her hand shaking.

'I'm afraid this isn't the usual sort of drinks party,' she began. 'I've asked each of you here because you are an essential part of a mystery. I think the best thing would be for me to read you something.'

Putting down the glass, she went through to the study and retrieved the letter. She looked across at Henry.

'This is the letter my grandma wrote. You gave it to me the day you handed over the keys.'

She turned to the others.

'Please, sit down.'

They did as she asked whilst she remained standing.

'It's only a short letter but when I've

finished reading, you will understand why I've invited each one of you here.'

Both Jack and Adam shifted uncomfortably. There was a sheen of sweat across Jack's forehead. Lara was reminded of Maria's words and quite suddenly her own nervous anxiety slipped away. She had a right to know the information each of these people had kept secret for years.

Emboldened, she unfolded the sheet of paper and read aloud Emma's words. When she had finished, there was dead silence. Adam spoke first.

'Where's George? Emma named him, too.'

'He wouldn't come.'

'He's a key part to this whole sorry mess,' Adam grated out.

'Perhaps we do not need George,' Maria said softly. 'Perhaps he thinks he has already said too much — hurt the people he cares for.'

'Keeping secrets is bound to be hurtful. It is never the answer,' Lara said emphatically. 'Please, we all know that each of us is keeping back a crucial piece of information, not just something piffling and unimportant, but vital, life-changing. I am asking each of you to speak out, to grant Emma's wish.'

Again, there was a heavy silence. The tension in the air now was almost tangible. They were all staring mutely at the floor.

In desperation, Lara said, 'Please, if they are not disclosed, these secrets will run on, possibly for ever. They're certain to spoil people's lives.'

No-one made a move to say anything. Lara's patience snapped.

'OK. I shall have no choice but to sell Mounts Cottage and go away. I can't live in an atmosphere of undercurrents and hypocrisy. But I'm asking you one last time, if you won't break your silence for me, do it for Emma. Please grant my grandma's dying wish.'

The atmosphere now was electric.

Henry cleared his throat, making them all jump. He lifted his left hand

and hitched his glasses back into place.

'I think it should be myself who makes the first confession. Whether or not the rest of you follow suit is, of course, up to you.'

He cleared his throat again and took a drink from his glass.

'This isn't easy, however, I should like to have been thought of as a man when it's my turn to go. So, I'm going to make a full confession now. It will take the weight from my soul for evermore. And believe me, keeping quiet is not an easy option, as you must all know. It corrodes, eats into your very core. I am going to be very selfish and tell the truth. That way I can drop this burden of guilt I've carried for most of my life.'

He took a deep breath and turned to Lara.

'My dear, you may have guessed but I want to tell you.'

'You are Teddy bear?'

Lara's voice was barely above a whisper. They smiled, an immediate link forged between them.

'That was Emma's nickname for me, yes. I was Emma's lover,' he said in a firm voice. 'Emma had my baby and she called her Esther.'

There were muted sounds of surprise but Henry swept on.

'I was sent abroad by my parents and never knew that Emma was pregnant. When I returned, she was already respectably married. I thought I was doing the gentlemanly thing by keeping quiet.' He put an arm around Lara's shoulders. 'But, thanks to the courage of my granddaughter, I can release myself from that vow of silence. I'm your natural grandfather, my dear.'

Happiness flooded Lara from head to toe.

'Thank you, thank you, for telling me. It's wonderful, like being given the most amazing present! I never expected to have a grandfather and it's just so . . . ' She buried her face against him.

'Why Teddy bear?' Maria asked roguishly.

Lara lifted her head. 'Let me guess . . . grandfather. Your office telephone number's an update of the original and you sign letters H. R. Jenkins. Would your middle name be Rupert?'

He chuckled. 'Now who's being perceptive?'

Jack stood up.

'Ladies and gentlemen,' he began, 'taking my lead from Henry here, I feel it is now my turn.'

A hush fell. Everyone looked at him expectantly.

'Twenty-five years ago, I betrayed my wife.'

Adam's face went paper-white.

'I was married and living down in Surrey but my father, Matt Branston, was running Pegasus stables. We came up now and again to visit. On one of these visits, I met Esther. On subsequent visits and also whilst I was covering the country driving to race-courses, I met her in secret. We fell in

176

love and had an affair. I suppose at this point you are all condemning me.'

He looked round at them. No-one spoke.

'But let me add something in my own defence. I was a young man then and my wife, Susan, whom I loved, was slowly dying from an incurable disease. I actually lost her long before she died. My friendship with Esther began as a support and comfort, and only later did it turn into love. When Esther discovered she was pregnant, she refused to disclose who the father was, not only to protect me, but to protect Susan. We were three people caught in an impossible situation. I am not excusing either Esther or myself. We both knew Susan wouldn't see Christmas that year and we decided to wait and get married after the baby was born, and we would have done, except for the fact that Esther died before Susan.'

Lara pressed a hand to her mouth, eyes wide with horror as she took in the implication of what Jack was saying.

'Lara,' Jack said, holding out both hands, 'come here.'

His voice was husky with emotion. She rose and went to him.

'What I am trying to say is, I lost both the women I loved, but Esther left me with the most precious of gifts, you, darling. You're my own daughter.'

Lara's knees buckled and she would have fallen if Jack hadn't caught her. Maria hastily fetched a glass of cold water and held it to her lips.

'You're my father?'

Lara could barely take in the staggering news. She gulped and cast an anguished look at Adam who was sitting with his head in his hands.

'I think, Jack,' Maria said chaffing Lara's hands gently, 'that before we go any further, I'd better explain the rest, don't you?'

For a moment he hesitated but seeing how distressed Lara was, finally nodded.

Maria said, 'Adam, you must prepare yourself for a shock.'

'Maria, I've had the biggest shock of

my life already. You see, I know about Jack being Lara's father. George told me on Wednesday night.'

Lara gasped. 'That's why you didn't want to face me.'

'Yes,' he said without looking at her. 'Can you blame me?'

'No.' Her voice was so low he could hardly hear it.

'And I thought nobody knew,' Jack said, fists clenched tightly.

'Esther told George,' Lara said. 'She was still conscious after the accident and it was George who found her.'

'All these years he's kept it quiet!'

'And there's something else he's kept quiet about, too,' Adam put in. 'OK, it's nothing to do with Lara, this secret, but since everybody's getting in on the act, I may as well confess as well. That way George will be released from a secret he has kept for me since I was six years old. Do you remember the fire up at Pegasus, about twenty years ago?'

'Do we?' Jack said with feeling. 'It took most of the barn and several stables were damaged so badly, they had to be pulled down and rebuilt. Matt was pretty well gutted, too.'

'Yes, and if he hadn't claimed on the insurance, he'd have been finished. Well, it was me. I started that fire.'

'What did you say?' Jack exclaimed.

'It was me, Dad. I started the fire, oh, not intentionally, I grant you, but it doesn't alter the fact that I caused all that damage and upset for Matt.'

Jack folded his arms across his chest. 'You'd better explain.'

'It was early afternoon, you know, the quiet time. In racing, all the staff get their heads down and have a sleep at that time. They have to. With early starts and coming back on for evening stables, believe me, they have to. Anyway, that day there was nobody about. I'd been digging in the garden, pretending to find buried treasure, as kids do. I'd unearthed a few bits of broken crockery, odd stones and stuff, and a very old piece of bottle glass. I'd taken all these treasures plus a comic and a bag of crisps and gone to play in the sunshine in the front part of the barn.

'Cutting it short, I found that angling the piece of bottle glass above my comic, with the sun's rays full on it, made the comic start scorching. Well, it was resting on top of the hay and the inevitable happened. The comic ignited. There was nothing I could do.'

He paused and looked round at them all.

'I was only six at the time. I can remember the flames going up in a big whoof and then I started screaming. But nobody heard me, nobody came, except George. He'd brought the eggs for Grandma. He looked after me, rang the fire brigade from the house and then went and woke Grandad Matt. He never told anybody how it started. They thought it an accident, and Grandad Matt claimed on the insurance. If I'd owned up that I deliberately started it, even innocently, he wouldn't have claimed, George reckoned. Matt's a man of principle. And, of course, without the insurance money he would have been forced to sell up. So, George and I kept quiet, until now.'

'No, Adam, it wasn't your fault.'

Everyone looked at Jack.

'It was my fault. Knowing Matt was in the house, albeit sleeping, I'd left you playing on your own. I'd taken the opportunity to go and see Esther. If it's anyone's fault, then it's certainly mine.'

'At least it's all out in the open now,' Adam said, holding out his right hand. 'Let's call it quits, Dad.'

Jack let out a deep groan as though he were in pain.

'No, no, it's not all out in the open. I've never been honest with you, Adam. Like Henry, here, I thought it was the best thing to do, to keep quiet. Now I see that it wasn't. I have to tell you . . . ' He struggled with the words. 'Adam, I love you as if you were my own flesh and blood, but the truth is, you're really my adopted son.'

Adam's jaw dropped. 'And Mum?'

'Oh, no, she's your natural mother. We married when you were less than a year old. Your natural father died in a car crash.'

'It's hard to take this in. All these years, the whole of my life, I thought you were my father.'

'But I am,' Jack's anguish was plain to them all.

Adam struggled to get a grip on himself.

'It will take a bit of time to sink in, but the one overriding thing I feel is relief, that you're not my natural father.'

Jack looked as though he'd been shot.

'No, I don't mean that how it sounds,' Adam said hastily. 'The relief is that I'm not Lara's brother, and I thought I was.'

The profound silence was broken by the sound of Maria laughing softly. Lara, trying to absorb everything that had happened, saw only the happy relief and love shining in Adam's eyes.

Striding across, Adam took her hand.

'I maybe premature in saying this, but somehow, I don't think I am. From Wednesday night, when George told me Jack was Lara's father, my whole world was shattered and turned into the worst kind of nightmare. I thought there was no solution to it. Now, suddenly, I find because Lara had the guts to get us all here tonight and bully us into coming clean, that everything has changed, except my feelings for her. And if she feels the same, and I'm fairly sure she does, we can go on from here, together.'

Almost shyly, Lara nodded.

'I'd like nothing better.'

'What a night!' Henry exclaimed. 'If you recall, Lara, I did say something to the effect of family relationships being the most complex. I didn't know the half of it.'

A gale of laughter followed his words and the atmosphere changed from tense and highly-charged to light and relaxed.

'I vote a toast to Lara,' Maria said, holding aloft her glass. 'Without her we would all still be stuck in a web of evasion and secrecy.'

'Here, here,' Jack seconded. 'Let's turn this into a celebration party.'

A roar of approval greeted his words. Right then a loud knock sounded at the back door.

A woman's voice called, 'Can we come in?'

'Who is it?' Lara put down her drink.

'Catherine.'

'Come straight in.'

But first in was Jodie who bounded forward, tail waving.

'Oh, my goodness,' Lara said worriedly. 'I'd forgotten all about Sophie. She's been gone ages.'

'Don't worry,' Catherine said following Jodie into the room. 'Sophie's here with me, and so is George.'

They both entered the room together.

'Blame me,' Sophie said carefully. 'I met George on Cuckoo Walk and he told me Bet was having puppies up at Pegasus. I twisted his arm to take

185

me to see them.'

'Have they all been born, Catherine?' Lara asked.

'Yes.'

Her smile was from ear to ear.

'Twelve little beauties.'

'Nay, lass, you've got that wrong,' George said.

They all waited, puzzled.

'Eleven little beauties, and one little runt, which,' he went on as laughter bubbled up all round, 'you've very kindly presented to me. He can't take my Gyp's place, but he can be my new family.'

Lara looked round at all the smiling faces and felt her heart fill with contented happiness.

'You're not the only lucky one, George. I've found what I was looking for, too — my very own new family.'